More, Please

Other Titles by Willow Summers

More, Please

BY
WILLOW SUMMERS

Chapter 1

───❧❧───

"**G**OOD MORNING, BEAUTIFUL."

My eyes fluttered open as dim sunlight streamed in through the windows. The air had that "early morning smell" that said it was way too early to have my eyes open.

Hunter stood by my bed holding a tray with legs. I could just make out a small white vase with a flower, and the rim of a glass. The smell of bacon wafted toward me.

"Hi." I rubbed my eyes, trying to get the sleep out. "What time is it?"

"It's five thirty. I need to drop you off at home on my way into the office."

"Why do you go to work so early?" I coughed, trying to wake up my vocal cords.

"I'm hoping I can actually concentrate today. I need to get some things ironed out for this takeover. Here, Mrs. Foster made you breakfast."

In another situation I might've whined about getting up, and then stayed securely under the covers for another fifteen minutes, but with a tray of breakfast being presented to me I wasn't about to complain. I scooted up and braced the pillows behind me, suddenly wide awake. "She must work really long hours."

Hunter's grin left me star-struck for a moment, as I took in his handsomeness. It was almost as pleasant seeing him first thing in the morning as having breakfast delivered.

"She must like when I entertain, which was why the late night, but she's usually here early."

Hunter put the tray over my lap and laid one of his shirts next to it. Then he leaned over and gently touched his lips to mine. As he was about to back away, he must have decided better of it, and connected a little more firmly. His hand touched the back of my head as he nibbled my lips, moaning softly. When he stood up, a small smile touched his lips again. "*That* I have never had." He brushed my hair back from my face. "A woman to wake up to."

He gazed at me with soft brown eyes for a moment longer. With another small smile, he gestured to my tray and turned to walk away. "Eat. It's getting cold."

I didn't have to be told twice.

As I ate, I reflected on my luck to have ended up in Hunter Carlisle's bed. Yes, he had problems, and some serious baggage in the form of a contractually obligated fiancée, but he was trying to open up. He'd admitted last night that he wanted to try and have a relationship.

I was all for it. Right after I ate breakfast.

A half-hour later I sat back and looked out the window, and finally decided I should get up. I'd thought Hunter would be encouraging me to get moving, but he'd gone downstairs shortly after delivering breakfast and hadn't returned. I figured I should be a big girl before he got irritated and said I couldn't come back.

I glanced at my pile of clothes, and then at his pajama bottoms and shirt. I should wear one set, but I wanted to wear the other. As it was my first time over here, and I really wanted to come back, I reached for my own clothes. Testing the boundaries would have to wait until next time.

I shrugged into my jeans, a pleasant soreness from last night acting as a reminder, and walked a few steps to glance in the mirror.

I flinched.

I had black smudges under my eyes, my hair looked like I'd stuck my finger in an electric socket, and one side of my face still had a light dusting of blush.

"After seeing this face, he'll rethink wanting normal." I cleaned myself up as best I could, using the tried and tested method of licking the pad of my finger and wiping it under my eye to remove the black. I tied my hair back and picked up my handbag.

All was quiet outside Hunter's room. I made my way downstairs, too shy to call out, as we weren't the only ones there. I didn't want to alert the fiancée to my whereabouts. He wasn't in the living room, nor in the dining room. I popped my head in the kitchen and found Mrs. Foster wiping down the counters.

"Have you seen Hunter?" I asked in a tiny voice.

She glanced up with raised eyebrows. "Oh. Good morning. Yes, he's in the library."

"Great, thanks." I turned to leave before remembering my manners. I turned back. "And thanks for breakfast. It was delicious."

"No problem, sweetie. That's my job." She smiled at me before returning to her task.

I should've probably brought down the empty tray. *Oops.*

I headed off toward the area of the house I hadn't seen to yet. I figured that was where I would find the library. As I got halfway down the hall, I heard voices raised in an argument. I slowed down.

"Blaire, I gave permission for visitors of a sexual nature—I did *not* give permission for sex parties. You can spend your time how you will, but in my house, there will be boundaries."

"Oh, really?" a girlie voice spat back at what was definitely Hunter. "As I recall, you didn't specify any of this in your precious *contract.*"

"If you look at the detail, you will see that I covered any acts that might reflect badly on my dealings in a social or business aspect. My housemate having wild orgies, participating in flogging, bondage, self-mutilation, among other things, is not something I want your strangers spreading around my circles of influence."

"Your live-in *housemate?* You arrogant prick! What

happened to *fiancée*?"

"This is a business arrangement, Blaire, between your father and mine. I went along with it to attempt to cut my father out of my life. This was understood in the negotiations that you sat in on. Since he has *not* been cut out of my life—he's more in it now than before this agreement—I'll be looking into a breach of contract."

"Is that right?" she snapped with a cutting and snide voice. "So let me get this straight. You won't fuck me, but you don't want anyone else fucking me, either? What am I supposed to do, take up a monk robe?"

I heard a sigh that was distinctly Hunter's. "I'm not saying to stop having sex, Blaire. I'm saying go about it with some discretion, or take it somewhere else."

"Somewhere else? I live here, too, *Mister* Carlisle. And don't think I don't know what's going on here. Your cook told me all about your pretty little piece of ass. She was trying to throw it in my face, the bitch. I'll bet that's the street trash secretary I've heard about, right? You're not only fucking the hired help, now you're bringing them around?"

I withered against the wall. I should really turn around and walk away. I didn't need to hear any of this. At the same time, the roadblock that was Blaire, and the contract she represented, was now very clear. She might not love Hunter, but she wanted him. She didn't sound like a girl that was happy not getting what she wanted.

"Watch yourself there, Blaire," Hunter was saying in a low and dangerous tone.

Blaire scoffed. "So it is her. That's your type, is it? Sweet and naive. I should've known. Men like you don't want sexually enlightened; you want the dumb little virgin that you can lead around by the nose. Well *fuck you*, Hunter Carlisle. If I can't have any fun, neither will you. If you keep bringing her around, I'll make your life hell, you got that? I'll show up at your business lunches, I'll spread nasty rumors around your social circle—if you try to trade me in for a troll like that, so help me God, you will rue the day!"

A beat of silence passed before Hunter said, "Are you done?"

"Not even remotely, you controlling piece of shit. Not even remotely." I heard the pounding of bare feet on wood before a wild-eyed woman emerged from the room along the hall. I sucked in a breath at her beauty. Hunter might've called it manufactured, but everyone else would call it model-worthy. Long blond hair framed her heart-shaped face in a series of waves. Her full lips, colored deep red, were currently pressed tight. Bright blue eyes and high cheekbones made her stunning. A long silk robe parted at the front, revealing a slim body with large, perky breasts and a cleanly shaved pubic area. She'd been fighting virtually in the nude. It hadn't slowed her down at all.

"Well, well, well. What have we here?" She slowed in her sensuous walk, not bothering to pull her robe closed. "If it isn't our deflowered little princess…"

I stayed frozen against the wall for a moment, terrified for reasons I couldn't explain.

"Come to find your master?" She stopped in front of me. Her hip jutted out.

I tore my eyes away from her bald pubic area, and then her exposed breasts. I really wasn't used to being confronted by naked people.

"Excuse me," I said, trying to slide along the wall like a coward, trying to sneak past. Her eyes shone with a maniacal flare that said she was capable of extremely damaging things. I didn't think rules bothered her, and I knew I would be the target if she decided to torch someone's house while that someone was tied up inside.

"What's sad is, you think he actually likes you. Let me fill you in, sweetheart. Hunter Carlisle doesn't like anyone but himself. He is a selfish bastard with a giant ego, and he wants a fixer-upper to drape across his arm to appear like one of the *people.* To seem like one of his workers. You're Cinderella for now, but you'll be old news tossed in the garbage when he has what he wants."

"Blaire!" Hunter's voice boomed through the hall-way. I jumped.

A vicious smile spread across Blaire's face as she beheld me. "Watch your back—I may decide to stick a knife in it. I would hate it to be a surprise."

She took a small canister out of the pocket of her robe and unscrewed the top. Turning toward Hunter, she poured a little line of white powder onto the skin between her thumb and forefinger. She threw Hunter a malicious glare before bending her head down and snorting up the line. She wiped her nose with her thumb before screwing the top back on the canister. She smirked. "Oops. Another rule broken."

With a last scathing look at me, she turned and sauntered away.

"I'm sorry about that," Hunter said in a troubled voice. "She's never been one to maneuver, but I'm starting to think her father was offloading her, rather than securing her a comfortable future."

"She's...precious." I tucked a flyaway behind my ear and leaned against the wall. "And she's always here?"

Hunter's gaze turned to me. He closed the distance between us and wrapped his arms around me, pulling me into his body. "Yes, unfortunately. She doesn't work, and she doesn't have a place of her own. Part of the deal was that she'd move out of her father's house and live with me. I think she thought I'd buckle and become a husband, of sorts. One like my father was. I've disappointed her."

"Then why doesn't she want to find someone else?"

"Money." Hunter kissed the crown of my head.

"So...you're locked in?" I couldn't prevent the hollowness in my voice.

Hunter squeezed me tighter. "I'll figure something out."

As Hunter led me to the library, my mind started whirling. He might be able to figure something out, but if that woman didn't get what she wanted, I'd be the first she'd blame.

I remembered the vicious, manic look to her eye and shivered. It was a pretty safe bet that she was capable of terrible, malicious acts. If Hunter brought me here again, she'd probably find ways to make trouble. I'd made a terrible enemy, one likely to be as unpredictable as she was dangerous.

Cold hands of fear crept through my body. I'd have to be on my guard, but would that be enough?

A LITTLE BEFORE nine, I walked toward my desk with my computer in hand. Brenda was just coming down the hallway with two cups of coffee. As soon as she saw me, a huge smile lit up her face.

"You're back! Oh thank God. I thought I was going to have to quit." Brenda set the cup down and sipped her coffee as she looked down at me. "Please say you're staying."

"Until he freaks out again, yes." I laughed as I booted up my computer.

"He was a *bear* the last half of the week. He sent one of those interviewees running from his office in tears." Brenda made her way to her desk. "Good. Bert will be pleased—did you see him?"

"Yes, he picked me up this morning. He said pretty much the same thing you just did."

"Oh yeah—when the big boss is in a bad mood, everyone gets it." Brenda set her coffee on her desk and glanced at the cup in front of me. "You better get that in to him, but then I want to hear how this happened.

Hunter Carlisle does not like to admit he was wrong. I hope you made him beg—that pisses him off even worse."

Smiling, I picked up his cup and headed into his office. The light streaming in was a welcome sight, as was the handsome man in the expensive suit looking at his computer. I put the cup down where I always did, and saw a grin crease his lips. He didn't look away from the screen, though, just like normal.

With a grin of my own, I started to walk away, glancing back when I was halfway out of the room. As he'd said at my mother's house, he was looking, watching my butt as I made my way out. He glanced up at me and winked before turning back to his computer.

When I reached the door, I heard, "Olivia…"

I turned back. His burning gaze hit me, full of command and power. "Plan on staying late tonight. I have some things I'd like you to do…"

Tingling with expectation, I left his office and settled in my chair, needing a moment before I started to tell Brenda the short version of why I was sitting in this office, and what kind of trouble I might have waiting for me if I tried to steal Hunter away from the woman that had signed a contract.

Chapter 2

———— ✦ ————

"DID YOU...WANT to see me?" I edged into Hunter's office. I'd pushed myself on him a few times, but this was going to be the first that was a little more...preplanned. I felt strangely sheepish about it.

His deep brown, hooded eyes looked up. His gaze raked my body, giving me pleasant shivers. A small crease formed between his eyebrows as he glanced at the clock. Regret took over his expression. "I've been called into a late meeting."

"Oh." I glanced at my watch, even though I knew the time. "Well, then..."

With sleek and graceful movements, he rose from his seat and came around the desk. I took a moment to admire his muscular frame and perfectly tailored, expensive suit.

"Time for a quickie?" I ran my hand up his hard chest.

"What are your plans after this?"

"I have no plans. Just home."

He traced my cheek with his thumb. His smoldering eyes delved into mine. "Come to my house tonight." It wasn't a request.

I hesitated. I did not want to encounter that crazy woman he lived with. "Maybe…my place…instead?"

"While I do love spending time in places as small as my closet, I'd rather not brave your roommate."

"My roommate is an ass, granted, but yours is bat-shit crazy."

He kissed my forehead. "I'll take care of Blaire. Stop at your house and gather whatever you'll need. I'll pick you up in an hour."

His deep timbre vibrated through my body. "Okay." I was entirely too complacent when it came to Hunter Carlisle. I couldn't do anything about it, though. The man had his hooks in me.

"Good." He leaned down, his lips grazing mine softly. Shocks of pleasure lit up my body as he nibbled my bottom lip. His large, warm hand slid from my chin to my neck, then down over my chest. He cupped my breast, kneading softly as the kiss intensified. His tongue entered my mouth, his hand leaving my breast and reaching under my skirt. I moaned as deft fingers danced up the space between my thighs. I clutched his shoulders as he cleared fabric away from my sex. Two fingers lightly traced along my slit, sliding my wetness over my clit before he started to massage.

"Oh," I breathed into his mouth.

My eyelids fluttered as his fingers moved and applied

pressure against my opening. I widened my stance, letting my hands roam across his chest, remembering that the door to his office was wide open. Anyone could walk in.

The thought thrilled me.

"Hmm, you're so wet." His deep growl rumbled hungrily.

I exhaled as two fingers worked into me. His thumb ran lazy circles across my clit, enhancing the pleasure, picking up the pace as my breath quickened.

"Yes," I sighed. My toes curled slowly as the pressure in my core intensified.

"Bring something sexy tonight," Hunter said in a husky voice, his finger-thrusting harder now. Faster.

Heat spread across my body. I gripped the back of his neck, holding his head down, my lips against his.

I was incapable of answering. Or kissing. All I could focus on was the delicious feeling of those fingers and the pulsing pleasure throbbing up through me. I moaned as my body tightened. I held my breath, feeling the unbearable height right before—

"Oh *God*!" I exalted, shuddering against him.

He smiled down at me. I couldn't smile back. All I could do was breathe raggedly for a moment as I came down. Shock waves of pleasure zinged through my body as he adjusted my panties and straightened me out.

"One hour." He kissed me and turned away, back to work.

"It's going to take me an hour to get home," I mumbled, trying to walk with legs made of Jell-O. Not that I was complaining.

Wiping the sweat from my brow, I made my way out of the office. Bert, Hunter's driver, wasn't out front—he'd probably gone home for the day—so I dialed the number for Hunter's car service. The bus would probably be faster, but getting chewed out by Brenda, and then Hunter himself, for not taking private transportation wasn't worth the aggravation.

Twenty minutes later I let myself into the small apartment I shared with Jane, a woman who really should know to pick up after herself by her late twenties. Sadly, that was not the case.

"You're home late." Jane sat on the couch in a faded, holey T-shirt. She had a bowl of ice cream in her lap and a smear of chocolate on her cheek.

"I'm always home late. My boss is demanding." I quirked my eyebrow. Since when did she start noticing my schedule?

I put my keys in the bowl by the door and made my way into the kitchen, ignoring the dirty plates stacked in the sink. None of them were mine. Call me stubborn, but I'd rather live in disarray than clean up after a grown woman I wasn't related to.

"Your rent check was on time. And here I thought this month would be your last…" Jane continued to look at me, an easy feat in an apartment as big as a shoebox.

"Yeah. Boss. As in, guy that tells me what to do in exchange for paying me."

Jane didn't respond. She also didn't stop staring.

Trying a little harder to ignore her, because it wasn't easy, I sulked off to my room as I thought about my options for that night. Thanks to Hunter's charge card, I had a bunch of sexy, lacy things I could choose from. But he was used to those. I wanted something that would make him salivate. That would make him lose control.

My mind went to the night I wore my old shirt. He'd practically jumped me. Naked was also an option.

He'd said something sexy, though.

After shoveling the mostly terrible dinner into my mouth, I did grab an old shirt, as well as some pajama bottoms. I also grabbed a silky nightie, a garter, heels, and fishnets. I'd see how the evening played out.

I stepped into the bathroom to grab some overnight products, like a toothbrush and hair product. As I made my way back to my room, Jane said, "Where are you going?"

"Not real nosy, are you?" I muttered.

"Huh?"

"Just going to stay with a friend."

"A new job and a new man, huh? Or are you fucking your boss? Because that is never a good idea, Olivia. But you needed a job, so I get it."

Wow.

Ignoring her was impossible. Wasn't going to happen.

I went back in my room and shut the door. Hiding was a safer bet. Otherwise, I might lose my cool and throw a frying pan at her head.

Everything packed, I sat and stared for a moment, wondering what I should do next, but then my phone chimed. A message from Hunter flashed on the screen. *"Coming up."*

A blast of excitement stole my breath for a moment as I jumped off my bed and grabbed my bag. I yanked open my bedroom door as a knock sounded.

"A little eager, aren't we?" Jane said in a droll voice.

Yes. Yes I was.

Knowing I was wearing the stupid smile of a lovesick girl, I ripped the door open and beamed at the incredibly handsome man standing in the hall.

"Hi," I said. It had only been an hour since I'd seen him last, but who was counting.

Hunter's sexy gaze paused on my face for a moment, which I knew was flushed with desire, before sliding past me into my apartment. That small crease in his brow appeared again.

He'd been in my apartment before, but had always been distracted. This was the first time he had been able to calmly look around.

"So it is the boss, huh?" came Jane's smug voice. She sucked so hard.

"Ready?" I asked Hunter, suddenly embarrassed.

"Yes," Hunter answered as he stepped out of the way, looking past me with a focused, power-filled stare.

Jane's eyes widened and her mouth snapped shut.

I needed to learn how to do that stare.

I stepped into the hall as he closed the door behind me.

"Sorry about the mess," I said in a whisper. If Jane heard me, she was liable to run into the hall to defend herself aggressively. "She...doesn't like to clean. And I don't like to clean up after her."

"How long have you lived there?"

Hunter held the door open for me when we reached the street. The cool blast of a San Francisco night greeted me as I stepped out onto the sidewalk. A black town car waited with its hazards on, double-parked.

"Way too long. It's cheap, though. And until lately, that was the only reason I still had a place to live. Thank you." I took Hunter's hand as he helped me into the car. "I cleaned up after my mom when I was growing up," I continued when he had slid into the seat on the other side. "I hate living in filth, but I'll be damned if I'm going to be someone's bitch. You know...if I'm not their daughter..."

Hunter didn't comment as the car pulled away from the curb.

"If you didn't work me so hard, I'd look for a place of my own." I smiled over at him, but he continued to stare straight ahead.

A weird tingle of uncertainty had me fidgeting with the hem of my shirt. I knew Hunter didn't care that I was poor. I *knew* this. He'd said it. But it was a hard fact to digest. From what I knew of rich people, they didn't like hanging around with those who weren't. My old boyfriend dumped me because he'd been embarrassed to have me on his arm. And he looked up to Hunter, so...

I blew out a breath. Insecurity: one of life's more irritating pastimes.

The car stopped in front of a giant house in the wealthiest part of San Francisco. The view was spectacular, overlooking the ocean and giving a glimpse of the Golden Gate Bridge.

Hunter got out as the driver opened my door for me. I hoisted my bag only to have Hunter take it from me, his jacket thrown over his shoulder.

"Is that all, sir?" the driver asked Hunter.

"Yes, Mr. Portsmouth. You can go."

"Thank you, sir."

I crossed in front of Hunter onto the sidewalk and up the path to his front door. After opening the door, he waited for me to enter in front of him.

"Did you eat?" he asked once we were in the foyer and the door closed behind him.

He put my bag at the base of the stairs. Soft light illuminated the hallway, enhancing his handsome features. The sweet scent of flowers from the arrangement on a small table tickled my nose.

His eyes delved into mine. "I haven't had dinner. I called ahead and had Mrs. Foster prepare something. Are you hungry?"

"I'd be hungry for Mrs. Foster's food anytime. If she's cooking, I'm eating."

"Such faith in her after only sampling her pot roast."

He put his hand on the small of my back and gently applied pressure, having me walk toward the kitchen.

"It was a really good pot roast."

"I take it you don't cook."

"I cook. Kinda. But I don't *cook*, if you know what I mean."

"I see."

He probably didn't.

He directed me through the richly decorated and spacious house and into the kitchen. He left me standing by a small table in the corner while he retrieved two covered plates from the oven. He set them on the center island, but then hesitated. "Would you like to eat in the dining room…?"

"Oh." I looked out through the archway, remembering the large, somewhat sterile dining room. "Can we just eat here?" I motioned to the worn table next to me.

"Of course." Suddenly fluid again, Hunter moved around the kitchen, gathering silverware, glasses, and wine with economic motions. He set two places on the table, opened the wine, set the glasses, and then retrieved the dome-topped plates. He set each down and stood behind a chair, looking at me.

"Are we going to say the Pledge of Allegiance, or…"

His brow crinkled. "Would you like to sit?" He pulled the chair back a fraction more.

"Oh, right. Sorry, I didn't expect the whole gentlemanly treatment at a kitchen table." I moved in front of the chair and sat as he pushed it in for me.

"If not here, where?" He removed the domes from the plates and set them on the island. I looked over the lasagna in the center of the plate. The smell wafted toward me, absolutely divine. He then poured the wine before taking his seat.

"It's just a lot of extravagance for a kitchen table. I'm not really sure what comes next." I laughed, glancing at him to take my cues.

"*Manga!*" With a grin, he picked up his knife and fork.

"What? You're not going to put my napkin in my lap for me? What kind of host are you…" I faked being put out as I slid my napkin out from under my utensils.

"I'm going to enjoy this, I already know it." I placed a morsel on my tongue. The flavors exploded, so much better than most of the restaurants I'd ever eaten at. A symphony in my mouth.

"Oh man," I said with closed eyes, just taking a moment. I needed a little quiet time to process how good this lasagna was. "She's a pro. No two ways about it."

When I opened my eyes, intent on getting another bite into my mouth as quickly as possible, I noticed Hunter staring at me. He hadn't taken a bite yet.

I gave my signature flush. "Sorry." I slowed my movements, lest he think I was a savage. "I haven't eaten this well for a long time. Not since my father cooked for me."

I chewed the next mouthful slowly. To try and dislodge his stare, I motioned at the table. "You eat here a lot, huh? Not at the big table?"

"I do, yes. It's usually just me, and it's usually out of economy."

"What do you mean, out of economy?"

He used both knife and fork at all times, something common Americans didn't. I generally switched hands for the fork when I needed to cut.

I eyed my knife, wondering if I should adopt the practice.

"I eat to live. I lift weights for fitness. I work to disappear from reality." He took a sip of his wine as his eyes lost focus. He glanced away. "You shame me, Livy."

"What for?" I asked around my full mouth. I really needed to go to charm school.

His expression turned uncomfortable. "You...*live.*" He nodded toward my plate. "I see how you're enjoying your dinner. The pleasure you're taking in it. I see the passion when you work on Bruce's project and know that, while I'm good at what I do, I don't feel that passion. I've...never really lived, I don't think. Not like you do."

"Oh." Warmth spread through me. I shrugged one shoulder. "Don't compare yourself to me. You have great cooking all the time, whereas I eat hotdogs and Top Ramen. You're doing your dream job, while I'm only just getting the chance to work on something I went to school for. We're just in different points in life. You were like this once, too, you just forget."

Hunter looked at me for a while longer, but didn't

share his thoughts. Instead, with a pensive expression, he turned his attention to his food. I noticed his movements slowed, though. He looked away to his left. He was tasting. Exploring the flavors.

I bit my lip to hide the delighted grin and tried to ignore the deep, warm feeling that grew stronger the longer I spent with him. My regard for him was flowering into something powerful. Something intense and profound.

I let out a big exhale. *Dangerous waters, Olivia.*

I took a sip of the wine to distract myself from a feeling that was quickly taking over me.

And moaned.

Hunter's eyes found me again.

"Sorry." I stared into the depths of that burgundy liquid. "But you also get some great wine all the time, whereas I get two-buck Chuck. Wowza. Good stuff."

"You're trying to rub it in my face now." His lips turned into a smile. He shook his head, glancing at the wine before going back to his dinner.

"Well, well. What have we here?"

I froze mid-chew.

Blaire stood in the doorway to the kitchen, glaring down at me like I was a filthy rat.

Hunter's gaze hardened. "Can I do something for you, Blaire?"

All hip and breast, the beautiful woman sauntered into the room with her arms folded. She glanced at my plate before homing back in on my face. "Didn't think to invite me to dinner, hmm?"

"We never eat together, Blaire. You're usually otherwise engaged." Hunter turned back to his plate.

"Yes, usually I am. Because *usually* you don't have time for anyone else. You work, you eat, you work out, you shower, you go to bed. So who is this Hunter Rochester Carlisle who brings home a *secretary*, I wonder..." Blaire leaned against the island, her face screwed up in scorn and hatred as she stared at me. "I warned you."

My throat tightened. I couldn't tell if she was talking to Hunter, or to me. She'd warned us both, sure, but I was the only one who might die from it.

"Blaire, as you know, the rest of this dish is in the refrigerator," Hunter said with a patient voice. "Mrs. Foster is always happy to make you a plate."

"Your hired help hates me, Hunter. They judge me, but for some reason, don't judge you. Now, why is that, do you think? You hire women to fuck you. You pay them to be your sex slaves. Yet *I* am the one being judged. Seems highly unfair."

Hunter put down his fork and turned in his chair to face her. Fire burned in his eyes. "We're trying to enjoy our meal. If your sole purpose is to cause problems, please see yourself out."

A flash of pain rolled across her face before rage covered it up. Her eyes burned just as brightly as his, but with a maniacal light. "I didn't invite anyone over tonight. I thought maybe we could be alone. But I see that you'd rather fuck the hired help." She pushed off from the island. "I tried to be nice, Hunter. I really did try. But now I guess I'll have to teach you a lesson."

She sauntered over and stopped right next to Hunter, staring down at him with hate sparkling in her eyes. "I don't like people making a fool of me, Hunter. It really doesn't sit well."

"I am not responsible for that."

She scoffed. "Aren't you?" Her gaze flicked to me before she slowly walked out.

When she was gone, Hunter turned back to his plate and stared at his food for a moment, his fists clenched and his lips thinned. He took a deep breath and picked up his fork. "I apologize for that."

"Should I go?" I asked.

His deep brown gaze hit mine, anger mixed with uncertainty. "No. You'll stay here tonight. I need to…take steps, however. I don't want you subjected to that every night."

Shivers covered my body upon hearing him speak like we'd be spending nights together in the future. Lots of nights. Maybe every night.

I smiled, and probably blushed, as my face felt suddenly hot. He must've seen it, because his eyes softened immediately. His gaze dipped to my lips again. "Finish up. I have to work out, but then I'd like as much time as possible kissing you."

AN HOUR LATER I stared down at the clothes I'd brought

for bed as Hunter used his workout room. I probably should've been in there with him, working off the brick of food I'd just eaten, but sometimes feeling guilty was much better than lifting weights.

I stared down at the shiny material of the slinky lingerie I'd brought. Then switched my gaze to the homely pajamas that I knew, especially in this mood, would drive him crazy. He'd set the mood when, after dinner, he came up behind me as I was rinsing my plate. He'd slipped his arms around my waist. He'd kissed my neck softly, stilling my movements. Without a word, he moved me to the side and took the plate from my hand. "Enjoy the rest of your wine. I'll clean up."

I smiled, thinking about it. He'd turned all domestic on me, so soft and subtle compared to the Hunter at work, but with the same current of power and command. There were very few men who could do both, but he was one of them.

Heat sparked in my groin as I let my fingers trail over the silky material on the right.

I'd feel sexier in that, with the garter and maybe even heels.

I glanced at the cotton pajamas again.

But he'd feel more comfortable, and maybe more open, if I wore frumpy pajamas.

I bit my lip, bracing my hand on my hip in indecision.

That was when I noticed the folded pile of clothes on the chair near the fireplace. His T-shirt and some light sweats—the very ones I hadn't put on that morning in case he got weirded out.

A smile graced my lips as I packed away what I'd brought. His clothes were the best of both worlds. I'd feel sexy for reasons it was hard to explain, and he'd get the domestic vibe he loved. Win-win.

I took off my clothes, *all* of my clothes, and stepped into his sweats. As expected, they fell down to the middle of my bare butt. I threw on his shirt, letting it drape over my body.

I looked like a woman in a Hunter sack.

I hoisted up the sweats and looked around for a way I could keep them up. A belt would look weird, especially since there were no belt loops, and using a safety pin would make getting out of them awkward.

With a frown, I looked around the room for divine inspiration. That was when I noticed the draft. There was a door open.

I'd closed the doors so I could get dressed.

I glanced up, half terrified I'd see Blaire running at me with a chainsaw and a hockey mask.

Hunter stood in a tank top, glistening and beautiful, his muscles on display with a sheen of manly sweat. A drop of liquid ran down his cheek and into his five o'clock shadow, rugged and gorgeous. His sweats clung in the right ways, hugging his muscular thighs and cupping his large manhood, currently starting to tent his pants.

He wiped a thumb across his lips as his eyes drifted

down my body. "Come into the bathroom."

The command in his voice sent shocks into me. I didn't even remember to add the "please." I was moving before I could process the words properly.

Chapter 3

———— ❧ ————

HUNTER TURNED AND shut his bedroom door before following me across the room. He threw a T-shirt in the hamper as he entered the bathroom behind me. As I turned to face him, I felt his strong hands on my hips.

He pushed me against the wall. His lips claimed mine, needy and eager, rough and commanding. He pushed down my sweats and ran his hands up the sides of my thighs.

I reached out for his shoulders, but he caught my wrists and pushed my hands up and out to the sides, bracing them against the wall. He was taking charge. This wasn't a time for sexual equality, it was a time for me to pleasure, or be pleasured, as he saw fit.

My chest tightened with excitement.

His tongue entered my mouth as he captured both my wrists in one of his large hands. I moaned as his hand slipped up my shirt and pinched a nipple. Shooting pulses of both pleasure and desire fired through me, pooling in my core.

He stepped back, grabbed the hem of my shirt, and ripped it over my head. He tossed it to the ground before letting his gaze travel my body once again. Taking another step back, he eyed me like a predator might. He pushed down his sweats and boxers. His large erection bobbed out, ready and eager.

"Turn on the shower to whatever temperature you want," he commanded.

Swallowing a lump of seedy desire, I opened the glass door to a large, square shower. I turned the knobs until I had the right temperature, only to step out and notice he was reentering the bathroom. The clothes were still on the ground, and he wasn't carrying anything, so I had no idea what he'd been doing, but the look of hot lust in his eyes left me with no time to dwell on it.

"Get in," he said in a firm voice, moving with that muscular gracefulness that had all the spit drying in my mouth.

I stepped into the warm spray, letting it coat my head and wet my hair. He stepped in after me, and despite there being plenty of room, he pushed me against the tile wall before reaching up to adjust the showerhead. The spray hit our bodies as he leaned down to my lips.

I chanced my hands on his shoulders. When he didn't push them away, I let my touch run along his collarbone and up to his neck before grabbing the back of his head. An urgency came over me that wasn't expected. I needed him, right then.

I pulled on the back of his neck, making the kiss

harder. He growled into my mouth, lifting my knee high. His body dipped right before his hard length seared into me.

"Oh," I moaned, my eyes fluttering.

His lips met mine again, sensual and passionate. He thrust into me, filling me up and hitting all the right spots. I moaned into his mouth as he thrust again, the tempo speeding up quickly. The warm water beat down on us as he rocked deeper into my body. It felt *so* good.

"Oh God," I said, everything tightening in my body to exquisite pain. "Oh—"

He pounded into me, holding my knee on his hip. Tingles turned into crashing waves of pleasure right before eruption!

"OH—!" An orgasm ripped through me, stealing my breath away.

"Hmm," he groaned, shaking against me in a climax of his own.

He slowed as the last waves of delight flowed through me. His kiss became lighter, but no less sensual. His head backed up, his deep brown eyes delving into mine. Something sparkled in their depths I couldn't make out. Without a word, he took a step back and ran his fingers through his wet hair and then down his face.

I shook out my arms. I felt all loose and tingly. Little bursts of pleasure still sparked through me.

I stepped away from the wall. And then my knees gave out. "Oh crap."

Hunter caught me against his perfect body. I

clutched his shoulders.

"You okay?" he asked softly, running his lips across mine.

"Yeah. Sorry. You took all the strength out of me."

He smiled as I straightened up. After watching me for a moment, probably to make sure I didn't swan-dive into the glass door of the shower, he grabbed a purple bath pouf and a bottle of Chanel body wash from the shower caddy.

"I'm not sure which is more ridiculous." I adjusted the temperature to a smidgen cooler. "A seriously muscular man using a girly purple pouf, or that he uses designer body wash. I mean, why not go for Dove? Save some money and match the pouf."

"This is for men." He held the body wash out for my inspection.

"And the pouf?"

"Mrs. Foster takes care of the shopping. Usually the pouf color is a secret."

"So, you're saying I've got the goods on you? Hmm." I tapped my chin. "How will I use such scandalous information…?"

He laughed, something I'd rarely heard him do, as he lathered up the pouf and moved my body into the spray. "Sorry, I should've told you to get your toiletries."

"I don't mind smelling like you," I muttered, a little embarrassed to make the admission.

The pouf slid over my body gently, followed by his hand. When I was lathered up, he washed the pouf and put it back. He then let his palms roam over me, kneading my breasts before massaging my back. His hand worked down and cupped a butt cheek before sliding to the other. His fingers ran down before rubbing between my legs, cleaning up the slickness from our lovemaking.

"You've got me hard again," he said, letting his lips drift down my neck. As evidence, his length slid between my cheeks and against my slit. "Let's lie down this time. I don't want you falling and getting concussed. Let me just clean up really quick."

With economic movements, he soaped himself before rinsing. I watched his hands drift over his mouthwatering body. White suds washed down his bumpy stomach, so deliciously cut. The muscles on his back and arms flexed and moved as he washed his hair.

He turned off the water and gently steered me out of the shower, placing me on a towel laid on the floor. With another towel, he dried me slowly before wiping himself down.

I grabbed the decorative green towel from the rack, and then paused. "I can use this, right?"

His brow furrowed. "Why wouldn't you?"

"I don't know. Some people like certain towels to be for decoration only."

"Go ahead."

He finished drying himself and walked out of the bathroom, tossing his towel into the hamper as he passed. I wrapped up my hair in a towel turban before following.

The lights had been turned off in the room. Five candles flickered romantically, placed around the room to spread out the soft glow. He'd even turned the bed down, folding back the comforter so as to make it more inviting.

"Since when does a mogul billionaire get all romantic?" I asked with a delighted smile.

"Since he met someone worth putting in the extra effort." Hunter led me to the bed. He kissed me softly. "But, I have to admit, I was in a different mood when I set this up."

I frowned at him and looked around. "What do you mean?"

Hunter stared at me for a moment before shaking his head. "I'll show you another time." He kissed me softly, backing me up to the edge of the bed. His hand wrapped around the back of my neck as his lips met mine. He leaned forward, making me lean back until I was scooting across the mattress. I laid my head on the pillow, our lips still connected.

"I just want it soft and sensual right now," he murmured against my lips. "I want more of those desperate whimpers."

His tip rubbed against me slowly before easing past my nether lips, taking the breath from my body. Sighing, I let my head fall to the side, focusing on the feel of him inside of me. Before I looked back at his handsome face, though, I noticed a black strip of fabric lying on the nightstand. Next to it lay a pair of handcuffs.

As my gaze went back to Hunter's eyes, darkened with desire, I remembered his commanding tone earlier. His dominating presence.

Heat ripped through me.

With him, it wasn't a question of if I'd let him, it was when he felt like it. I trusted him implicitly.

He must've read that thought in my eyes, because a slow smile curved his shapely lips. "Another time."

I noticed it then. The seriousness in his gaze as he moved within me. The tone to his passion. His eyes were so soft. So deep. Emotion rode his movements. He'd welcomed me into his home, he'd shared his past, and now he was connecting with me in an extremely intimate way.

I wrapped my arms around him, feeling the heat. Feeling the intense emotion. My body ramped up, hard and fast, needing him. Craving his touch.

"Hunter…" I kissed him harder, the pleasure mounting. It burned through me. "*Oh!*" An orgasm dragged me under, drowning me in bliss.

"Oh G—" I squeezed my eyes shut as waves of ecstasy rolled through me. His body shuddered.

As the shock waves subsided, leaving me in a pleasant glow, he shifted to the side and then curled around my body protectively. His hot lips kissed my neck softly. I fell into the moment, feeling the warmth swelling. Knowing what it meant.

I sighed and snuggled deeper into him. "Beds are good."

Hunter squeezed me just a bit. "Well said."

I chuckled. "I think Blaire is probably going to kill me. Seriously. She's crazy. What were you thinking?"

"She can't hurt you. She's just a spoiled child that only got attention from a nanny growing up. Like me."

"You seem…a lot better adjusted."

"I'm not, Olivia," he whispered. "I function, and I earn my way, but how many men do you know who employ women in place of a relationship? I'm not as spoiled, or as violent, as Blaire, but I'm just as delusional about what I can have in life. And so far, like her, I've had everything I've wanted."

"To a degree," I said.

His silence hinted that he wasn't sure what I was talking about, or that maybe he didn't agree. "You still have your dad in your life, and we both know *that's* no fun. You lose battles with the board a third of the time. And you couldn't outfit your plane with that hideous red carpeting you were after. So no, not everything."

He nuzzled my neck, making warm fizzles crawl up my middle. His arms tightened around me. "And soon, when you realize what a shallow bastard I really am, I'll lose you."

His tone was light, almost playful, but I heard the edge in it. The insecurity.

"As soon as you realize what a psycho I am," I replied, "you're out the door."

He squeezed me again. "Not likely."

I snuggled back into him with a smile. "You're not a

shallow bastard, Hunter. You're a rude one. Someday you will say *please* all the time. I have faith."

"Again, not likely."

"Challenge accepted."

Chapter 4

THE NEXT DAY I arrived at the office at my usual time. Hunter had once again dropped me off at home insanely early, as that was when he went to the office, leaving me to sleep for another hour before I got ready for the day and lugged myself in.

"Morning." Brenda set Hunter's coffee on my desk.

"Good morning. Anything pressing for today?"

"For me? Yes. For you? I have no idea. He has you doing harder stuff these days. Bet you wish you hadn't let him know how smart you are..."

I smirked as I opened my computer, then grabbed Hunter's coffee as my machine booted up. "Shows what you know. I like being busy."

"Busy and harassed are two different things. You're just too young to know it."

"Jaded!" I accused.

"Yeah. One step ahead of you."

I laughed as I let myself into Hunter's office. As usual, his attention was focused on his computer. I put his coffee on the corner of his desk, where I always did, and turned to walk away.

"Olivia."

"Yup?" I turned back.

"I have a business meeting in the city at the end of the week. Dress is business casual. I'll require your presence." He leveled his commanding business stare at me. "I've emailed you."

I quirked an eyebrow. Telling me like this seemed a little heavy-handed. "Okay…"

He turned back to his computer.

What the hell?

Screwing up my face in confusion, I turned with the intention of finding that email. It was obviously super important for him to call this much attention to it.

"And Olivia…" he said as I was halfway to the door.

"Yeah?"

He was still staring at his computer. His hand was braced on his mouse, his finger raised, as though he was just about to make some important, life-altering click.

The man was in a strange mood, to say the least.

He said, "My mother is having a dinner party in a couple weeks. It is…not business. I wondered if you would accompany me. I'd like you to meet her."

Hunter Carlisle was asking me to meet his mother! Holy crap!

My first instinct was to squeal. Luckily I didn't. That would've been ridiculous. Instead, I wiped the hair away from my face with the back of my hand and batted my eyelashes.

Only slightly less ridiculous.

"Sure. Yes, of course. I would love to. Will you be telling me what to wear to both occasions?"

He glanced at me, a sparkle lighting his eyes. "I'd like to say no, but…"

"I don't have any fashion sense, I know. For a guy so heavily into fashion, I have no idea why you don't have more gay friends."

"That's a stereotype, and I don't have any friends," he mumbled, his shoulders tensing.

I waved him away. "I'll leave you to your pity party, then."

As I left his office, I couldn't help a delighted smile.

"What?" Brenda asked as I sat down. "You look like he just gave you a gold bar."

"Kind of did. Wants me to meet his mom."

Brenda's eyes widened. Her cup lowered slowly. "Well ho-ly crap. What did you say?"

"Yes, obviously. What do you think I said?"

"Knowing you, I have no idea. Wow. His mother, huh? That's big news."

"Yeah. I probably shouldn't be this giddy, since he still maintains he can't love, and he's a shallow monster, but…I am."

Brenda huffed and turned back to her computer. "He's a drama queen. I assume you aren't taking that seriously?"

"Mostly. But he's in a dour mood. Beware."

"That's his default. I'm well used to it, my dear. The way he's been smiling lately makes me worry that he's unbalanced. I wonder if he's about to go postal."

"You two have a strange relationship."

"It's not me, it's him."

I smirked and clicked into my inbox.

BY THE END of the day, my sexy systems were fired up, knowing spare time usually meant Hunter naked. I walked into his office with a sure step and excitement bubbling up.

He sat at his desk as normal, the setting sun casting long shadows that reached across the office floor. He looked up when I approached, his gaze flicking to the cup of coffee in my hand, and sliding over my body.

"Last call," I said with a husky voice, reveling in his handsome face and broad shoulders. "I'm ready to go. Do you need anything?"

His brown eyes were trained on me, deep smoldering fire. I set his cup on the corner of his desk, ready to strip. Equally ready to pleasure him. Or myself. Or us both.

"No, I'm all set. See you tomorrow."

I felt like I'd been dunked in a pool of icy water. My body went rigid. He didn't even want to see me later?

"Oh." I shrugged before swishing my hair off my shoulder. "No problem." I gave him what I hoped was a confident smile. "See you tomorrow."

His gaze lingered for a moment, probably assessing, before turning back to his computer.

What the hell?

The walk back to my desk was a confused one. He'd been all mushy last night, he'd asked me to meet his mom, and then…he sends me home alone?

In the grand scheme of things, this wasn't a big deal. We weren't even dating. Not really. There was no reason why I would spend every night with him.

I kinda wanted to, though.

Half pouting, I grabbed my computer and headed toward the elevator. I hated this part of a new relation-ship—or whatever it was we were doing. The wondering. The questioning. I should have just asked him why he didn't want to spend every waking moment with me…

I huffed as I got into the elevator. Yeah, that'd go over real well.

THE NEXT FEW days went exactly the same. He didn't strip me, didn't demand to be undressed, and he didn't invite me over. He gave me an assessing look, and wished me goodnight. He was treating me like a buddy. Not even a buddy with benefits!

I was definitely in the insecure girl stage of the rela-tionship, or whatever this really was. By the end of the week I was a ball of stress, so when I found myself outside the building, waiting for Bert, I hadn't expected the "Hey!" out of the blue.

I jumped and swung around with a pointed finger. "Hah!"

My friend Kimberly walked toward me with a sensuous gait, loosely curled hair spilling over her shoulders, and a quizzical smile. "Why are you pointing at me?"

I dropped my finger as a blush crept into my face. "Sorry. That was my attempt at defense from an attack."

"Pointing and laughing is your natural defense against attackers?"

"I wasn't laughing, I was shouting. Apparently that scares people away."

"If it does, then you're not doing it right…" Kimberly laughed. "Where have you been?"

I gave her a belated hug in hello. "Working my tush off! I'm so sorry I haven't returned your call—I've been wound up so tight."

"It's fine—" Kimberly cut off as Bert pulled up in the sleek black town car.

He heaved his sizable girth out of the driver's side and walked toward me with a grin. "Ready?"

"Oh." Kimberly backed up a step.

"Do you want to come over?" I asked Kimberly, wanting to clutch her and drag her regardless of her answer. I hadn't seen her in a while, thanks to the job and Hunter's emotional sabotage, and missed her.

She shrugged, smiling at Bert. "Sure. I have a few hours."

"I have to get ready for a business meeting…dinner…thing, but you can pick out my clothes. You like that sort of thing."

Kimberly laughed as she followed me to the car. Once we were both tucked in, she said, "So you get a ride to functions?"

"I have to take the car everywhere, actually. Hunter doesn't trust public transportation and yet he trusts cabs, for some reason. When his car service is busy and Bert is off, he wants me to cab it. Apparently having no witnesses doesn't worry him."

When we got to my apartment building, I asked Bert, "Are you picking me up, or who do I call?"

"Mr. Carlisle will be around to pick you up."

"Ah. You get to go home on time. What's the occasion?"

Bert got out of the car with us, holding the door even though he hadn't been quick enough to open it. He shrugged his huge, meaty shoulders. "I think he's using the limo tonight. He probably wants to impress these business guys."

I scowled. Brenda had said the meeting was more of a formality than anything. Everything had been hashed out behind closed doors. This dinner was to shake hands and celebrate the contract that had been signed. They called it a meeting, but it wouldn't be in any meaningful sense.

"Huh." I shrugged and waved at Bert as I made my way into the building, Kimberly on my heels.

"So what have you been up to, Miss Busy?" Kimberly asked as we climbed the stairs.

I gave a world-weary sigh. "Long hours, number one."

"Yeah. Part of the job…"

"Plus, this guy Bruce—whose company we're buying—has a project I'm working on. It's just for fun at the moment, but at the rate we're going, he's thinking we have a moneymaker. So he's talking about partnering up for that."

"Is that the guy who offered you a job?"

"Yeah, but I turned it down. Well…kinda. I said I'd work on it in my spare time while I worked for Hunter full-time."

"Do you have time?"

I let us into the blissfully empty apartment.

"Not really. But it's really fun. And great experience. More up my alley, you know? Besides, it's really hard to say no to Bruce. He's just so passionate about creating and programming—it's great working with him."

"And what's going on with Hunter?" She settled on my bed with a beaming smile.

"Don't get comfortable just yet—you have to pick out my outfit!" I opened my closet door and invited her to take a look. Hunter had given me leave to dress myself, amazingly.

Which had added fuel to my crazy fire.

"Oh." She bounced up.

"He's… We're…" I slumped onto the edge of my bed. "I don't know. It was going great—you know, but then…"

I told Kimberly the whole story, from his fears, to Blaire, to his strange indifference this last week. "I don't know what's going on and I'm afraid to ask. I know he doesn't think he can love, but we're so close. Closer than he's been with anyone in a really long time. I just don't understand how he could just shut it off."

Kimberly settled on the bed next to me and gave me a firm hug. "You didn't say the L-word, right?"

"No way! Are you kidding? He'd run away screaming. And plus I don't…" I let that thought trail away as I analyzed the deep and intense feeling deep in my gut. I thought of how much I liked talking to him, and how lonely I'd been this past week without him.

My stomach flip-flopped. Oh crap.

"What?" Kimberly asked, watching my face.

"Nothing." I was not going to admit the extent of my feelings. Not until I had a better grip on them.

"He's probably just busy and stressed out, like you are." Kimberly rubbed my back with a supportive smile. "Seriously, Livy, the way he acts with you—that man can never have taken a woman home. Not ever. And he's taken you home *twice*. That means something. Just give him time."

I massaged my shoulder, working at the tension knots in the muscles. "I'm just worried that if I give him too much space, he'll forget what it's like being with me, and be okay giving me the boot."

"That's because you're a woman, and we're hard-wired to think into things too much. Guys don't spend their lives thinking about this stuff. Trust me."

"And then there's his crazy fiancée to worry about… That chick is cracked."

"She sounds…" Kimberly hesitated.

"Bat-shit crazy." I nodded. "She is. She's crazy. But she sounds like a scorned woman. I might end up like her."

"No you will not!"

I laughed at her indignant reaction. "I think she likes Hunter, but he doesn't give her the time of day."

"Can you blame him? I mean, she signed a contract to marry him. From what you just said, he wasn't shy about his lack of regard for the situation. She was deluding herself."

"Aren't I, though?"

Kimberly gave me a hard stare. It was the "I am running out of patience for this" stare. "He didn't make you sign a contract, he has taken you home, and he *asked you to meet his mom,* Olivia! He likes you. What more proof do you need?"

"Ugh!" I flopped back on my bed. "I know. I know. But it's just weird that he didn't want anything to do with me this week."

"He probably thinks it's weird that you didn't want anything to do with *him* this week. Goes both ways."

"Stop making sense. It's ruining my mope."

Kimberly laughed and lightly slapped my thigh. "Let's pick you out something to wear so you'll look fabulous. Looking good always cheers me up."

She started swishing through the clothing in my closet. She paused on a dress as she said, "But the Blaire situation…I'd be worried about that."

"I am. She has a bunch of money. She can pay peo-ple to...I don't know. I'd say slash my tires, but I don't have a car."

"Just watch your back, Olivia. I'll see what I can find out about her."

I did not like that Kimberly was telling me to watch my back. It meant a lot of my fears were probably true.

Chapter 5

———— ❧ ————

"**Y**OU LOOK GOOD. No—stop messing with it!"

Kimberly swatted my hand away from my hair, a sort of half updo with curls and hair spray and bobby pins. It was so firm and riddled with hair spray that it felt like a wig, yet somehow it still managed to look loose and natural. Kimberly had a gift.

Regardless of how it looked, though, I felt like I was going to prom. All I needed was a gaudy bracelet of flowers and I was all set.

"When's he supposed to be—"

A knock sounded at the door, cutting Kimberly off. She gave me an excited smile and followed me into the living room.

"That for you?" Jane was in the kitchen, making herself something to eat. She looked me up and down.

"Yeah, I got it." I opened the door to Hunter. He stood with a black button-up shirt hugging his delectable body. His gray pants showed off his trim waste. His hair was in that contained messy style he did so well, and his face was shaved clean.

My heart started pounding as I looked at his handsome face. "Hi," I said in a breathy voice.

"Ready?" That hooded, smoldering gaze, reminding me of our sweaty bodies entwined in ecstasy. It had my knees going weak and warm tingles spreading through my body.

He glanced behind me. "Hello, Kimberly. Nice to see you again."

"H-hi, Mr. Carlisle. I was just helping Livy get ready." Kimberly tucked a lock of hair behind her ear with a bright red face. Desire shone clearly in her eyes. It was something most women couldn't help in Hunter's presence.

"You did a great job. She looks beautiful."

I smiled like an idiot and walked forward, taking his arm.

With Kimberly following behind, we descended the stairs and out through the front of the building. Once there, Kimberly said, "Okay, well, I'll talk to you tomorrow, Livy."

"Do you need a ride somewhere?" Hunter asked as he gestured toward the double-parked limo. The driver stood in front of an open door, not at all concerned about the traffic congestion he was causing.

"Oh, that's okay. I'm not far from here." Kimberly smiled up at him before giving me a little wave.

"I'll call you tomorrow," I promised.

Hunter led me to the limo and handed me in before

crossing to the other side and climbing in.

"How do you always get in my building?" I asked once he was settled, determined not to let my anxiety over his behavior show tonight.

"I had a key made."

Shock widened my eyes.

His smile was evil. "That's not true. The last couple of times I showed up as someone was leaving. I got lucky."

My exhale was noisy. "Good. I think that would skirt the line between flattering and creeping out."

"You look beautiful, Livy." He took my hand. "I'm sorry I haven't had time for you this week. I've had...things on my mind."

And just like that, all my wondering melted away. "It's okay. I did a bunch of work for Bruce."

"Yes. He said. He's pleased with your work."

"It's fun." I bobbed my head, hoping I hadn't showed my discomfort throughout the week. As the limo slowed in front of one of the prominent, swanky hotels in San Francisco, I switched to business. "So, we're just supposed to smile and shake hands in this thing?"

Almost immediately, Hunter's expression closed down into one of importance and indifference, and he looked out the window at what awaited him. When the limo stopped, he stepped out of the car. My door opened a moment later, the limo driver waiting right beside it so I could get out.

As I joined Hunter on the sidewalk, his hand connected with the small of my back and directed me up toward the entrance. "You won't need to say much. Dinner will consist mostly of men congratulating themselves, trying to ease off the stress of the price we settled on. Afterwards, we'll head to the bar and put in some face time."

"And I needed to come...why?"

"Because I wanted you to be with me."

A thrill coursed through me as Hunter opened the door and followed me in. We went through the grand hotel to the dining area a level down. I turned my smile and glittering eyes on, and my brain off, as we entered a sea of suits with only a few women.

"Someday, I'll be at the head of a company despite my sex," I mumbled.

"Yes, you will. In the meantime, keep your eyes open and your mouth closed. Watch how the top people interact with each other—what language they use. That way, when you're in a position of power, you'll know how to best communicate to get what you want."

"I also need to learn how to play golf."

"Watching baseball and football wouldn't go amiss, either." Hunter's hand left my back as a gray-haired man with a bright smile and too-white teeth approached.

"Hunter Carlisle! So glad you could come!"

I let patience envelop me in order to endure the night.

TWO HOURS AND a delicious meal later, I found myself

waiting for Hunter to get us some drinks. He'd chosen the location: a booth mostly obscured by a velvet curtain, nestled into a corner as the hotel's way of using all available space. He'd done his time chatting and socializing, earning plenty of pats on the back, but he never once smiled. No one seemed to have minded.

"Room for me?" Hunter showed up at the table with two drinks and tight eyes. He wasn't having the time of his life either.

"Yup." I slid over so he could sit next to me. He placed my cosmo in front of me and sipped his scotch.

"How long do we have to stay?" I asked, glancing out past the curtain to the laughing and jeering businessmen.

"I'll make one more appearance when I go get a refill, then we can go. I've taken the liberty of booking us a room here. I hope you don't mind."

"Oh." I looked down at my outfit to hide the relieved smile of him wanting to spend the night with me again. "I didn't bring a change of clothes."

"I've had that taken care of. I have something I want to show you tomorrow."

"About work?"

He sipped his scotch again, his eyes pointed out toward the business melee. "I plan to work from…home. Tomorrow."

The hitch in his voice, and the strange uncertainty in his tone, had me looking at him more closely. A small crease had formed between his eyebrows, and I didn't think it had anything to do with this meeting. Before I could ask, though, I felt his hand sliding up my thigh. The fabric of my skirt bunched at his wrist.

My legs spread of their own accord. I had no control over it. I also had no control over the moan that resulted from his fingers tracing down my panty-covered slit.

"People might see," I whispered with my eyes closed, doing absolutely nothing to dissuade him in any way.

"I know." The heat in his voice sent shivers down my spine.

I spread my legs wider, feeling reckless and aroused. His fingers dipped into my panties, rubbing along my wetness, before plunging into my body. I moaned again, leaning against the table as the strength went out of me.

"Sit on my lap," Hunter said quietly, taking his hand away so he could undo the buttons on his pants.

Red-faced and on fire, I glanced out toward the public. "Hunter! *Here?*"

"Yes. I need you. Right now." With a hand on my shoulder, he gently pushed me toward the wall, scooting with me. When we were in the most secluded place possible, the push turned into a pull, coaxing me onto his lap.

"Oh my God!" I said excitedly, glancing out toward the melee again.

The booth was large and the table was small, so there was plenty of room to maneuver, but still!

"I can't do this…" I bit my lip. Desire lit me up, naughtiness made me squirm in expectation, but the fear of getting in trouble had me hesitating.

"Olivia, let me remind you that we are at a work function. As such, you are under a verbal contract to give yourself to me whenever I require." His tone had dropped into that deep, commanding tone that vibrated through me. "I want to fuck you. Sit on my cock."

I exhaled as my desire burned. "Holy heavens."

Before I knew it, I was positioned over him, sitting in his lap with my skirt pulled up my back and my panties moved to the side. His hard, bare length rested between my wet, aching slit.

"That's better." His hands roamed up my chest and cupped my breasts. "Rise up."

I did as instructed. I felt his tip run along my wetness before pausing at my opening.

"Sit," he ordered.

I lowered my body back down slowly. His girth pushed past my lips and into my opening, filling me, chasing the breath from my lungs. My thighs hit his, lodging his manhood deeply within me.

"Now rock against me, Livy." He put a hand between my thighs. His middle finger rubbed my clit as I rocked forward, feeling him slide deep within me.

Sweet sensations mingled with the thrill of doing this in public, heightening the pleasure. I tried to keep my eyes open, keeping lookout in case anyone should wander up, but it felt *so* good.

"Faster, Olivia," Hunter breathed.

I sped up, stroking him with my body and exalting in the feelings. His hand on me kept pace. Heat curled within my core before unfurling.

"Yes," I said urgently, focusing on his hand, on his deep slide, on the thrill of the moment. I leaned forward as instinct replaced logic. Fear of being discovered only heightening the pleasure. I lifted and came back down, hearing a smack as my thighs slapped against his.

"Hmm," Hunter said, his movements on me turning coarse. Harder.

That pushed me higher.

Panting, I rocked my hips, occasionally rising up and slamming back down for the jolt in pleasure. I bit my lip to keep from moaning. My core tightened. My breath hitched. His fingers played over me expertly.

"I'm going to—" A climax stole my words. The breath rushed out of me as my body blasted apart.

Hunter shook in orgasm beneath me, leaning against my back as my movements slowed down. Taking deep breaths, I shuddered as shock waves vibrated through me.

He nuzzled into my neck as we came down, still holding me tight. "Even a moment after I'm with you, Livy, I want you again. It's constant."

I wanted to ask why he'd stayed away from me the week before, but I didn't want to ruin it. Instead, I closed my eyes, soaking in his embrace.

He straightened up then, and moved me off him. "We'll have one more drink and then get out of here."

Chapter 6

THE NEXT MORNING I stepped out of the shower and into the kind of bathroom only the best hotels could boast. A fluffy white robe hung on a hook for me, which I took after I mostly dried off, and wrapped my hair up in a towel turban.

In the cool air of the temperature-moderated room sat the closet, full of a new wardrobe I had neither picked out, nor needed to return. Hunter arranged for his people to outfit me in exact sizes, and in colors and cuts that suited both my body and my complexion.

Or so Hunter said when I had marveled at the wardrobe the night before.

"Have the documents arrived?"

I looked into the main area of the suite where couches stood in front of a large TV hanging on the wall. In the corner, Hunter sat at the desk with his laptop open and his cell phone held to his ear. He'd been that way since the small hours of the morning.

Realizing he wasn't talking to me, I ducked back into

the bedroom and took my place in front of the closet, marveling at all the finery. As it was Saturday, jeans and a shirt would be perfect.

I picked through the selections, the equivalent of a week's worth of clothes, only to find there were no jeans. Scowling, I looked again. Nope.

Disappointed, I chose a pair of slacks instead, as well as a top that was way too nice for a weekend.

The dresser had all new underwear, with lacy bras and panties as well as standard cotton fare. I chose lace, because really, at the price Hunter paid, it would probably be more comfortable even than the cotton.

When I asked why Hunter stocked the room as though we'd be staying a while, he'd tilted his head in confusion and said, "There was no telling what you'd want to wear, so I had my assistant get everything."

Everything except jeans, apparently.

I spent time brushing out and blow-drying my hair, and putting on a light dusting of makeup. That was the problem with nice clothes—a messy ponytail and plain face didn't really go. I had to at least *try* to look pretty.

After that, I visited the safe, struggling not to be uncomfortable as diamond earrings, tennis bracelets, and all manner of gems glittered at me. I didn't really want to put any of these on. They matched the clothes, but there was no telling what I'd do to them. I might scuff a ruby, or accidentally lose an earring, or…who knew? I wasn't practiced in wearing expensive things—I didn't know how to take care of them.

I reached forward anyway. Hunter wouldn't take my fear as a viable reason to refrain from wearing his purchases. He'd just tell me to start practicing.

After I chose the plainest of the options and fastened them on, I stood in front of the mirror. I now looked like a richer version of myself, and I had to say, the transformation was great. I felt like a princess.

If only I could relax at the same time. This just wasn't Saturday attire.

I walked out into the main room as Hunter set his phone on the desk and went back to his computer. I barely stopped myself from plunking down in the couch as I might have done in jeans. Instead, I sat almost gracefully. I crossed one ankle over the other. Then uncrossed, because I didn't feel like being dainty.

"What's wrong?" Hunter asked, still staring at his computer.

"Nothing. Why?"

"You're sighing loudly." He swiveled in his chair and dropped his arm over the back. His sexy gaze took me in. "You look great, apart from the scowl. What is it?"

"Do you never wear normal jeans?" I blurted.

He glanced at my slacks, and then the flats I'd chosen when I would've rather had Toms or Sketchers. Hunter's fashion assistant needed a reality check.

"You feel too dressed up."

"Very astute, Mr. Carlisle. You've solved the riddle."

The corners of his mouth tweaked upward. He turned back to his computer, closed it, and then slipped it into his computer bag. He stood, dropping his phone into his pocket. "Shall we go? We'll do the errand first, then you can take me shopping and dress us both like street urchins, if you want."

"Street urchins...?" My scowl etched more firmly in my face. I stood. "I didn't see anything to pack up all the clothes. How are we supposed to get them out of here?"

"The assistant will take care of it." He slung his computer over his shoulder and came toward me.

A flash of warmth stole my breath away. I reached out for him before I knew what I was doing, just wanting to touch him. His lips touched mine softly. He opened my mouth with his, flicking his tongue in playfully. His arms came around me, holding me tight. He had my toes curling right before he backed off a bit.

"Let's go," he said softly, loosening his hold.

"What's the hurry?" I ran my hand up his chest.

"This situation is temporary. I want to figure out something...a little more permanent." He kissed me again before stepping back.

Not knowing what he meant, but completely on board, I half stumbled toward the door before I realized what I was doing. "Right." I glanced around, feeling like I was forgetting something. I was about to leave a hotel room without anything in my hands. It just felt weird. "What about my clothes from yesterday?"

"The assistant will grab everything."

"Who is this assistant?" I asked, doing one more sweep. I almost wanted to take the robe just to have *something* in my hands.

"She only just started. You'll meet her soon. Ready?"

I walked out of the room, glancing back furtively. "Why the new assistant?" I asked as we made our way to the elevator.

When the doors opened, a smiling attendant greeted us. He waited for us to enter and then pushed the button for the ground floor. He clasped his hands in front of him and pointed his face demurely at the ground.

"I need certain things looked after. How are things going with Bruce?" Hunter asked as the elevator chimed. "We didn't get a chance to discuss it."

Yes, because you were in the middle of a personality change.

When the doors opened on the right floor, the attendant put his hand out to ensure we weren't caught if they randomly closed, and said, "Have a good day, sir, ma'am."

"Thank you." I smiled at him. Then, when out of earshot, I said, "It feels weird that the hotel doesn't trust its patrons to operate an elevator."

"It saves us from having to keep an elevator assistant on staff." His voice was colored with humor.

"Sure, joke, but know that this hotel is basically calling you an idiot. They don't trust you to push the right buttons. They probably assume you poor rich sods will be riding the elevator all day, not sure how to get out. That, or you'll be wandering the halls, lost, calling out for your assistants…"

Hunter laughed. "Or maybe they're using the flattery of a helper to create another job or two."

My eyebrows lowered, because while I didn't think that was strictly true, it was certainly a perk for the work force.

"How's it going with Bruce?" Hunter repeated as we stepped out of the hotel.

I allowed myself to be steered to the right, where he handed a ticket to a man at a small podium. "Great, actually. I have a bunch of stuff I need to do later today. Or tomorrow. But it's fun work, so I don't mind it."

"More fun than being an office assistant, huh?"

I grimaced, because it was. It was in my field, whereas what I was doing for Hunter was not even remotely close to what I studied in school. I loved learning new things, but I also loved programming.

"He's half thinking of getting another business going," Hunter said as a sleek sports car pulled into the carport in front of the hotel.

A man in uniform stepped out and hustled over with keys. Hunter slipped him a tip as he stepped to the passenger door and opened it for me.

"Arrive in a limo, leave in a supercar. You need a team of assistants." I smiled at him as I sat in the plush leather seat.

"I *have* a team of assistants," he replied before he closed the door and walked to the driver's side.

"I doubt his wife will be thrilled with him starting another business," I said as Hunter steered the car out of the hotel's carport.

"He plans to keep it small this time."

"There's no way." I shook my head, checking social media on my phone as Hunter drove. "He thinks big, like you. He'll start small, but as soon as that gets rolling, he'll reach for more. You wait."

"Yes, he will. I've been…advising him. If he reaches in the right way, and organizes things properly, there's no reason why he has to do the heavy lifting when things escalate. He can maintain creative control, company control, and stay married."

"So you're taking over already?" I snorted.

"Just advising. He has to come up with a project first."

"Which he will. The one we're working on will seriously rock. Seriously."

"He'll need investors…"

"He's rich. He'll probably just fund it himself," I argued.

"At first, sure. But it's a big risk, and advertising is expensive. It'd be better to gamble with a larger company's money. At least until the ball is rolling."

I glanced up as we hit the crest of a hill and started down. The ocean sparkled in the distance with the sun beating down on it, the winters in San Francisco often better than the summers, and the day lending proof.

"We're not going to your house, are we? I don't really want Blaire yelling at me today."

"We won't be seeing Blaire."

It was a non-answer, and I didn't much like the elusiveness of it. He didn't take her seriously, and it would probably earn him a knife in his back. For me, it'd probably be an axe to the head. The less I had to deal with that woman, the better.

"Well, we're only a few months away from putting our game in beta testing. If that goes well, we can get it live in no time."

"And then the work really starts."

"Not for me. I'm just the laborer. I don't have anything to do with the business end of things."

"You will."

I rumpled my eyebrows at the conviction in Hunter's voice. We slowed into a turn. Thankfully, it was taking us away from his house. A few minutes later, he turned into a driveway of a three-story building. The first story appeared to be just the garage.

"Who lives here?" I asked in confusion.

The garage door rose. He pulled into the cavernous space and shut off the car. The door started lowering behind us.

"Is this the hideout for your secret drug cartel or something?" I asked as I got out of the car. "Are there going to be topless women in there cutting and bagging coke?"

"You watch too much TV."

As we entered the house, I noticed the tightness in his eyes and the rigid set of his shoulders.

What was going on?

He started up the stairs, his gaze everywhere at once. He checked out the freshly painted wall, the banister, the steps themselves, and the ceiling. On the landing, he brought out a key before glancing at the second set of stairs leading to the third floor.

He fit the key in the lock and clicked it over. I expected him to step aside and direct me through the door, but he didn't. For the first time since I'd met him, he stepped in ahead of me.

Warning bells went off. Blaire and villains and homicidal clowns could've been waiting in there for all I knew.

"Are we in danger?" I asked in a hush, following him in a hunch. I was ready to run and I didn't care who knew it. The first sign of danger and I was out of there.

Hunter's gaze took in the polished wood floor of the entryway that turned into a hallway to the back of the flat—because this was, indeed, a flat. Not an apartment, like I lived in, where there were a few units per floor. This was one living space that took up the whole floor of the building, with another flat above where someone else lived. And judging by what I could see so far, it was *huge* by San Francisco standards.

"I'm thinking of buying this building, and wanted your thoughts," Hunter said as he took two steps to the right and stood in the mouth of an archway.

"Oh." I straightened up. "Why didn't you say so? I was thinking the worst." I put my hands on my hips and checked things out.

A large kitchen opposite the entryway had granite counters and all the latest appliances. A mat graced the ground in front of the sink, and the wine rack in the corner was fully stocked.

"Does someone live here now?" I asked as I moved through the spacious kitchen and into the dining area on the other side.

A large table, set with crystal and china, was set up in front of a filled china cabinet. Off to the right of that, in the front of the flat, crouched a sofa and chairs looking on a large entertainment system and huge TV.

"Not at the moment, no."

"So whose stuff is this?" I circled back around to the door, Hunter dogging my steps.

He didn't answer me. Instead, he put out his hand toward the back of the flat. "The bedrooms are at the back."

Weird. And since when did he need a second opinion? His way was always the right way, regardless of the logic involved.

It occurred to me that often houses being showed were staged with furniture and decorations, though this one didn't have anything on the walls. Those usually came with a realtor passing out information.

Although Hunter would probably bypass that.

I passed a bathroom with a new sink and vanity unit, and glanced into an empty bedroom opposite. This one looked out into the atrium, a hollow in the middle of the building letting light in. At the back were two more bedrooms, one a master with a huge bed, curtains, a TV, and other fine things, and the other bare. Beyond those rooms was a large balcony with stairs leading into a backyard.

"There's an en suite bathroom off the master bedroom." Hunter pointed into the room.

"I have no idea what the value of flats are out here, Hunter," I said, stepping back into the hallway. "I don't know how I could possibly help you."

"Do you like it, though? Does it fit your tastes?"

"*My* tastes?" I shrugged, looking around again. "I mean, yeah. It's really nice. Renovated and spacious. You could get a pretty penny in rent, even though it's way out in the Richmond District."

"Would you live here?"

"If I was in college, had plenty of money and good roommates, sure. I'd brave public transportation for this place."

"Only if you were in college?"

I walked back to the living room before glancing at the kitchen. "If I had a family I would, too. Although I doubt I'd want to raise a family in the city, personally. But if I did, this would be a great place. Otherwise, I'm getting too old for roommates."

"Why would you need a roommate?"

I planted my hand on my hip and gave Hunter a leveling stare. Sometimes talking to a man who owned his own island was exasperating. "This place is *huge,* Hunter. Even if I could afford it—and with prices in this city, I doubt I could, not even with the huge paycheck you write me. And there's way too much space. I'd use a quarter of it, *maybe*. I'd end up dusting and cleaning a giant place I'd only use a little bit of. Doesn't make sense for a single person."

He stared at me with a blank expression, as though prompting me to come up with another, more reasonable assessment. Realization dawned on me.

"You've already bought this place..." I wasn't sure if I was accusing him or just completely mystified.

"Yes."

"And had it updated and furnished..."

"Furnished. It has already been renovated. A cleaner is scheduled to come every month—more, if you need it. The new assistant is not only highly competent, she can cook. She'll take care of all your needs. It's still in escrow, but I was given leave for you to start moving in."

"Wait..." That wasn't quite the conclusion I had come to. "*My* needs?"

I looked around again, this time with wide eyes. "Are you smoking crack? I can't live here!"

"Why? The place you live in now is filthy and tiny—you're not happy there. You were planning to move anyway. I've solved the problem."

"You've become my keeper."

His brow furrowed. "How so?"

With an open mouth, I stared at him. Sometimes the man was just dense. "I can't afford this place, Hunter, which means you don't plan to make me pay. Which means you are putting yourself in charge of my living arrangements."

"Your landlord is currently in charge of your living arrangements, as is your current roommate. What's the difference? Consider it a perk of the job."

"But you'd have a key..."

"Yes. And I will use it when I want to spend the night here."

Shivers went down my spine. He stared at me with that hot, commanding gaze, sucking out my will to resist. I shook my head slowly, feeling the desire to give in take hold.

"I don't need a *quarter* of this space," I muttered. "And it's so far away from downtown. Getting anywhere will take forever..."

"With Blaire making things difficult for you, you can't stay with me until I deal with her. I can't stay in your place, for obvious reasons. This solves those problems. You will take the car service when you need a ride, or use your own transportation, which we'll pick out next weekend."

He stepped forward, his eyes dark with arousal. His arm snaked around my middle and pulled me into his hard body. "I don't know if I can give you a future, Olivia. I'm not sure I can keep you happy long-term. But I'm going to try. For you, I'll try anything. That is my compromise. This place, that I can visit anytime, will be yours."

I looked deeply into his eyes. The heat in my middle

swelled and overflowed. "What happens if all this ends?" I asked in a breathy whisper, lost in his smoldering gaze. "Where do I go?" It had to be asked.

"You can stay here forever, if you want. This is yours. Upstairs will be a home gym. The extra bedrooms can be offices or whatever you want. This building was purchased for your use for as long as you need it. Change any of the furnishings—you have unlimited spending. Make this place your home."

His dominating gaze and the heat in his voice had my sex aching. The last of my strength to resist melted away. "Okay."

He bent to my lips, his kiss passionate and deep.

"What does the bedroom look like, again?" I asked in a needy voice, running my hands up his chest.

Chapter 7

H E WASTED NO time in getting me to the other end of the flat, his hands peeling away my clothes as mine ripped at his. We backed into the bedroom, lips connected, urgency hurrying our movements. I yanked his shirt out of his slacks and pushed the fabric over his broad shoulders. His perfect chest greeted me. I worked his pants down next, my breath speeding up as he undid the buttons on my blouse. When my bra fell away, he leaned down and fastened a hot mouth to my nipple. I moaned softly, running my fingers through his hair. He straightened up and shoved down his boxers, probably intending to flip me on the bed next, but I had other plans.

I dropped to my knees, taking the base of his erection in my fist and running my tongue over his tip. I sucked him in, fondling his balls with my free hand. As I withdrew, I stroked to the accompaniment of his soft groans.

I sucked him in again, withdrawing faster this time,

pumping my fist in time with my efforts. I bobbed over his hard cock, taking him deep in my throat before letting up, increasing the speed to match his breath, his flexing muscles, and his groans.

"I want to come inside you, Livy." Hands grabbed under my arms and hoisted me up. His length popped out of my mouth.

A moment after standing, I was falling again, hitting the mattress with a bounce. He was between my thighs immediately with his mouth, pushing my legs apart so he could lick up the center of my heat. His mouth focused on my clit as two fingers dipped into me.

I moaned and bucked into him, already needing him inside of me.

He must've sensed it, because he climbed up my body in a hurry. His hard chest raked against my taut nipples, sending shooting pulses of pleasure through my body. He braced his hands under my knees and pushed my legs high on his waist, angling before plunging deep inside of me.

"*Oh* God," I said in surprise, not expecting the sudden depth from the position.

He slammed into me, hard and fast. His mouth covered mine in a bruising kiss, spiraling me higher. I clung to him, gasping and panting with each thrust. His body crashed into mine. My core tightened and shivers racked my body. Before I could even get my bearings, suddenly the world spun, as an orgasm ripped through me.

"Oh!" I shouted, arching back.

"Hmm," Hunter moaned, shaking with his own release.

His movements slowed, became languid. His lips trailed down my neck and back up, sliding along the bottom of my jaw. I was still panting with the climax, but his soft ministrations started building me again. His slow movements pushed my pleasure higher.

"No." Hunter pushed up from the bed, looking down on me with a face shining from fatigue. He shook his head. "No. Don't start up again."

"*Me?* You're the one still kissing me all sweetly!"

His mouth turned upward as he straightened. "You're so damn sexy, Livy. I orgasm and immediately want you again. It's…distracting."

"Hmm. So what now? Do you have a lake you want me to look at, or something? A beach? Maybe a summer home in the Hamptons?"

"I have work to finish up. I can camp out at the dining room table, if you don't mind…"

"Only if you're naked. My house, my rules."

He gave me a full smile, making me blink up at a man so handsome it should be outlawed. He could have any girl he wanted. *Any* girl. What was he doing with me?

"What happened?" he asked, pulling me closer. He ran the back of his hand over my cheek. "Where'd the smile go?"

"Sorry. Just blinded by the sun. Which is your beauty. It'd be a really good place for a Shakespeare quote, actually. I just sound stupid."

"She is beautiful, therefore to be woo'd. She is woman, therefore to be won," he said.

I leaned in to him, slipping my arms around his waist. "Smart and hot. Did it hurt?"

His eyes sparkled, probably knowing what was coming. "Did what hurt?"

"When you fell from heaven. Did it hurt?"

He kissed my forehead. "No, actually, because I climbed up through hell."

I laughed as he stepped away. "Meet you at the kitchen table. No clothes, right? That's the deal?"

"Correct. Except I don't have my computer."

Hunter paused at the door. He looked back at me. "I'll have your assistant bring it over. You need to meet her anyway."

I watched his muscular butt move away, pleasantly distracted for the moment. When he was gone, I looked around. Then shook my head. The man was insane. He had bought a whole building—two flats and a garage—just to have his crush close. Money was nothing to him, granted, and real estate was a great investment, especially in this city, but he hadn't done this for anyone else. Not even for his fake fiancée. In fact, instead of putting her here, trying to get her out of his hair, he had bought it to give me a nicer place to live. He was thinking of me more than himself. He was a really, really good guy.

And I loved him.

I blew out a breath and just stood still for a moment.

Holy shit. I loved him.

Obviously, yes, I knew it was coming. I knew I was on the road to *l'amour,* but actually realizing I was there…

With a guy that didn't think he could properly love…

Well, I'd been in worse situations. Might as well just ride it until it bucked me off like all the others.

"I've really stuck my foot in it this time."

Chapter 8

———∞———

"A LITTLE LATE today..." Brenda said.

I glanced at Brenda as I passed her desk, slightly harried and fully prepared to blame it on Hunter if he got mad at me. I set my computer up and noticed the cup of coffee on the edge of my desk. "I moved out to the Richmond District. It takes *forever* to get in here now. I had no idea seven miles would take that long."

"Nice place, though, right? You can thank me for finding it."

"He had you scouting last week, then, huh? The papers must have gone through in record time. I had no idea things could move that quickly."

"They can when the buyer is sitting on a pile of gold." Brenda turned in her chair and surveyed me full on. "It's getting serious between you two..."

I shrugged, dipping a finger in the coffee. Lukewarm. "You couldn't take this in to him?"

"He doesn't like to see me. He likes to see you. So if I take it in, he downs it so you'll bring him another. That man does not need more caffeine. He needs a hit on a bong."

I smiled, getting up to get a fresh cup. "We're not getting serious, no. We're the equivalent of dating, I think. I'm not sure that he wants to know how I feel…"

"Ah." Brenda leaned against her desk. "No, probably not. He's a bit closed off." She turned back to her computer. "You'll figure it out. It's nice to see him happy. At least what passes for happy, anyway."

I rolled my head to loosen my neck as I got him a fresh cup of coffee, grabbing one for myself as well. He'd stayed over last night, and whether it was a good idea or not, I had spent the night with my head on his chest, savoring the feeling of his arm wrapped around me. It had been really great at the time. My neck wasn't so great this morning, though.

After setting my cup on my desk, I walked into his office, noticing the light spilling over his features and highlighting his ridiculously handsome face. It was a view I loved seeing every morning.

As I set down the cup, he glanced up with a quirked brow.

"What?" I asked, bracing my fist on my hip. I was ready for it.

"Lose your way this morning?"

"It wasn't my idea to move so far away."

His eyes sparkled as he looked back at his computer. "The takeover of Bruce's company is moving quickly. I wouldn't be surprised if he starts hounding you to get the work done on his side project…"

"Oh." I relaxed my tense shoulders. I'd been ready for a fight—I had to simmer down now. "It's fine. Since you work so much, and I live in the boonies now, I'll have plenty of time in the evenings to get to it. Janelle is working on outfitting the extra rooms with offices."

Janelle was the new assistant Hunter had hired for me. A woman in her early forties, she was efficient, great at working on her own initiative, and one helluva cook. I absolutely loved her. Even though my instincts screamed at me to not accept yet another thing from Hunter, I just couldn't send her away.

Besides, I had created a job by keeping her. That was what I kept telling myself, anyway.

"Did you give notice to your old roommate?" Hunter asked in an even tone, clicking on an email that came in as we were talking.

"Janelle is drafting it today. She said she'd deliver it, too. She's in the process of moving all my stuff to the new place. Your office will have a bed in it, by the way. For people who come to visit."

"My office?" Hunter glanced back at me, a small crease between his eyebrows.

Uncertainty churned in my stomach. "Th-there was the extra room, so I figured I'd put a desk in it for you. You know, so you don't have to sit at the kitchen table like you did over the weekend…"

He stared at me in silence for a moment before turning back to his computer. I stood awkwardly, not sure if

I should say something further. I didn't want him to think I was asking him to move in or anything, but I did have that extra room, and it had plenty of space...

I opened my mouth to explain, but then closed it again. The man had bought a building for me—buying him a desk with his own money and putting it in the spare room wasn't a trip down lover's lane. If anything, it was a nod to him for purchasing the building in the first place.

Without another word, I about-faced and walked from the room. I wouldn't tiptoe around him. It wasn't my style. Mostly.

"Okay, then," I said, returning to my desk.

"Atta girl!" Brenda exclaimed, not bothering to look over.

I crinkled my brow as I got to work. She had randomly cheered me on for no reason. I kind of loved it.

IT WAS A little after noon and I'd just decided to get myself a sandwich when I heard, "Incoming," in a low voice.

I glanced over at Brenda, wondering what she was talking about, when I caught sight of movement coming our way. I glanced at Hunter's schedule, seeing he had time blocked off for a couple hours.

"Do I need to stay?" I asked, clicking out of the calendar. Scheduling meetings and looking after the guests was something that fell under Brenda's jurisdiction.

Before Brenda could answer, blond hair in loose curls

framing a beautiful face caught my eye. A high-dollar tailored suit wrapped around an incredible body, the skirt reached her the mid-thigh revealing a shapely and tanned leg.

Blaire.

Cold washed through me as her eyes hit mine. She smirked in a condescending way as she stopped by Brenda's desk. Beside her stood a tall man in an equally expensive suit carrying a briefcase. He looked expensive and important, and screamed *lawyer*.

"I'll let Mr. Carlisle know you're here. Please have a seat," Brenda said in that frosty way she had when she first met visitors. Hunter couldn't have done it better himself.

Blaire flashed me another condescending smirk as she sauntered toward my desk. "So." She ran her finger along the edge as the man with her walked away toward the seating area. "Working girl, huh? How's the *boss* treating you?"

"Great." I pointedly looked at my computer, pulling up a spreadsheet I was working on to have something, *anything* to do instead of having to talk to her. My stomach rumbled, but there was no way I was going to get up and walk out. Not while she was playing the intimidation game. I had to stand my ground.

"He hasn't come home the last couple nights. I heard he bought his new mistress a flat. How quaint. You must feel like Cinderella."

"Big words, coming from someone living in his

house with nowhere else to go…"

Oops. I hadn't meant to say anything. I did not need to stoop to her level. Nor did I need to incite rage in a crazy person.

"And at least *I* have a ring." She rested her hand on my desk. The large diamond on her ring finger glittered in the light. "I haven't put much effort into seducing him. I figured he'd come around on his own. But based on your prancing around him like a dog in heat, it seems I have to up my game…"

Do not respond. She wants you to respond. Don't do it!

I clenched my jaw, staring at my spreadsheet.

"I'd be worried, if I were you…" Blaire smirked.

"He'll see you now," Brenda said, standing from her desk. She gave Blaire a frosty look as she passed, pausing in Hunter's door.

Blaire smirked at me again before leaning down. Her expensive-smelling perfume wafted by my nose. "Watch yourself, little girl. I know where you live now."

She straightened as the man she was with passed her. With a soft laugh I could only describe as terrifyingly evil, she followed Brenda and the man into Hunter's office.

My release of breath was a noisy affair. I slumped against my desk.

"What a bitch," Brenda whispered as she closed Hunter's door. "She's here to try and keep Hunter in that stupid contract he signed."

"Does she have a shot?"

Brenda paused by my desk. She looked down on me with the sparkle of anger in her eyes. "*She* doesn't, no. But I heard Hunter talking—the problem is with his father. There was an exchange of inheritance on the premise that Hunter would marry Blaire. I think whatever Hunter's dad had going with Blaire's father mostly fell through or didn't work out—I don't know the details. But Rodge has to agree to release Hunter of his liability."

"And he won't because he knows Hunter wants him to."

"Exactly. If Hunter breaks the contract, there will probably be millions in damages. Millions. It would cripple Hunter financially."

"I thought Rodge married Hunter's mom for money because he didn't have any…"

"His business was in trouble, and then yes, he got a bailout. But then he made the most of it. Now he's worth a pretty penny."

My heart sank. "Hunter will probably have to go through with it."

Brenda's expression turned comforting. "Don't underestimate Hunter. He can be sneaky when he wants to be. He'll figure out something."

I endured Brenda's pitying gaze as she settled at her desk. "Looks like he wants a witness," she said a moment later. "Not that I blame him." I caught her closing a PM before she grabbed a notepad and got to her feet.

As she let herself into Hunter's office, I couldn't help but reflect on the situation. Hunter was sneaky and extremely intelligent, but Rodge was those things as well as being cunning and malicious. If it came to a battle between father and son, I had a feeling the father would win. Rodge would be holding a grudge, since Hunter had secured the takeover from Bruce. He wouldn't want Hunter to have another victory.

TWO HOURS LATER, the door to Hunter's office opened in a swirl of anger and perfume. Blaire stormed out, heels punching the floor with each step. She paused in front of my desk, beautiful despite her red face and lips pressed together in anger. Her nostrils flared as they stared down at me. "You won't win. I'll make sure of it!"

I stared up at her, trying to keep my face blank and composed, as the man with her laid a hand on her shoulder.

She shook him off, staring down at me in rage for another moment, before turning and stomping off toward the elevator.

"Spoiled little brat," Brenda said when Blaire was out of earshot.

I couldn't help a small smile. "She didn't get her way, I take it?"

"Not at all," she said in a whisper. "It's exactly as I said earlier. She has not got a leg to stand on. Plus, get this…"

Brenda moved to the front of my desk, glancing at Hunter's open door for a moment. She lowered her voice even more. "Her dad cut her off. Well, kind of. She gets an allowance, but her trust fund has almost dried up. She needs to marry rich, but word's gotten around of how crazy she is. Her dad won't give her another penny, and he doesn't care about the contract with Hunter because the business with Rodge has also dried up. Not a leg to stand on…"

Brenda turned up her nose with a smile, tapping my desk. "Serves her right."

"But Hunter still has to go through Rodge."

Brenda shrugged as she made her way to her desk. "He'll figure it out."

AT THE END of the day, I shut down my computer and lugged myself into Hunter's office. He was turned toward the large wall of windows behind him, looking out on the sunset.

"You okay?" I asked quietly, stopping by his desk.

"Come here, Olivia."

I walked around his chair and paused by his knee, looking down on him. He took my hand and pulled gently, placing me on his lap. I leaned against his chest, running my thumb along the stubble of his chin.

"Blaire wear you out today?"

His arm came around my waist. "No. If anything, that was a victory."

"Brenda said your dad was standing in the way of you getting out of the contract."

Hunter's hand rubbed up my back and around to my collar line. Deftly, he undid the first button. "Yes. He is.

He's given his requirements for releasing me from the contract without messy litigation."

My next button popped open. His hand trailed down my middle.

"What's that?" I asked as my breath sped up.

Hunter opened another button. Then the last. He pushed my blouse open, exposing my see-through, black, lacy bra. His lips softly met my neck as his hand cupped my breast. It seemed he didn't plan to answer me.

"Hunter," I said.

I barely heard his release of breath. His hand fell to my knee. "He wants to take you on a date."

I stiffened.

"He wants a date, and he wants to take you home and spend the night with you." Hunter leaned his forehead against my chin. "He wants this because he knows I would never allow it. He wants to tarnish you in my eyes."

I struggled to find my voice. "What happens if you say no?"

"I fight the contract, of course. In truth, I'll stand to lose a lot of my wealth. I don't care about giving my inheritance back, but he worked a lot of damages into the contract. It's like he knew this would happen. I'm only telling you because I don't want you hearing it from Blaire or my father."

"He wanted the upper hand regardless of your decision..."

"Yes. He's always been one for strategy."

"How long will you have to be married to Blaire?"

Hunter shook his head, putting his hand to my jaw softly. He looked up at me, his eyes soft. "I won't marry her. And I won't give you to my father. I'll fight it. Fortunes can always be rebuilt."

Tears came to my eyes. "I can't let you do that for me, Hunter. I won't sleep with Rodge, but I won't be the reason you lose everything, either."

"Shhh." Hunter pulled my head down, brushing his lips against mine. "Don't worry about it. I'll figure it out. You're mine—I won't give you up. And I won't make a fool out of you by marrying Blaire and keeping you as a mistress. You're better than that. You're better than me and my fucked-up life. I'll fix this somehow, Livy."

His kiss deepened as his hand fell to my breast again, kneading softly. His fingers played across the swell before pausing at the clasp in the center. A quick flick had it popping open. He pushed the fabric to the side before breaking the kiss and leaning across me, taking one of my nipples in his hot mouth.

I sucked in a breath as his hand fell between my legs. His fingers ran down my panty-covered slit, wet with need. He rubbed the top in a circle while sucking my nipple. Pleasure heated my body, pulsing through me.

"Bend over the desk," Hunter demanded softly. He helped me off his lap before standing up with me. His eyes were soft yet smoldering, filled with desire and longing both. "I need to be inside of you."

I walked to the desk and bent over, feeling my ardor

rise. I felt him behind me, his legs brushing up against mine. Palms started mid-thigh and pushed upward, moving the fabric of my skirt up and over my butt, exposing my lacy thong.

A brief pause almost had me looking back before I felt a hot mouth against my panty-clad sex. I moaned as his hands landed on my knees, coaxing my legs wider apart. I complied eagerly. Fingers hooked around the fabric covering me and pulled it to the side. A scorching tongue licked up my center.

"Hmm," I moaned, laying my cheek against his desk.

His touch disappeared. Cool air assaulted what a second ago had been blasting heat.

A zipper sounded.

My heart started to beat faster as I waited for him. Bent over his desk, exposed, anticipating what he would do next.

Clothing rustled. A blunt tip made a trail down my aching sex.

"Oh, Hunter," I said, my lips fluttering with the delicious contact.

The tip stopped at my opening. Light pressure had me pushing back, wanting the thrust. Wanting him deeply inside me. His palms braced on my butt, though, keeping me pinned.

His erection barely pushed past my lips, then stopped.

"Please, Hunter," I said. Shivers spread fire through my body. Tingles heightened the expectation, promising exquisite pleasure. "Please…"

More pressure, entering me slowly. Not enough.

"Deeper," I moaned, clutching the desk in desperation. "Deeper, *please*, Hunter. Fuck me!"

Agonizingly, the tip pulled out. It slid along my pounding sex, teasing.

"You're mine, Olivia," Hunter said in a hoarse whisper. "I won't ever share you or give you away. Not for anything, do you understand?"

"Yes," I whispered.

His palms slid over my butt and up my back. His chest lay on top of me. A hard thrust had him pushing deep into my core.

"Oh!" I exclaimed as his thighs hit mine.

"You're mine," he whispered again, his mouth to my ear. He crashed into me then, hard and dominating. Each thrust was like a shock of pleasure, exploding through my body.

I moaned and writhed, shoved against the hard wood desk with each thrust. Our skin slapped together. My body wound up, incredibly tight.

"Oh, God," I exclaimed as the friction vibrated through me. "Oh, God. Oh my *God!*"

He pounded into me, unyielding. The sensations grew, expanding. Larger. Overcoming me.

"Oh Hunt—oh Go—" Words failed me. My teeth clicked closed. My jaw clenched. Colors burst behind my eyes and a *boom* of orgasm rocked my body.

"Olivia," Hunter groaned, shaking over me. His

hands gripped me tightly.

He leaned over me more heavily as I panted against the desk, both of us quaking in the afterglow. He kissed my cheek softly with his hands braced around me possessively.

There was no way in hell I would sleep with Rodge, that was for sure. But I had to admit that part of this was my fault. I'd been integral in getting Bruce to Hunter's side, and Rodge knew it. I was a part of this issue. A big part.

I had to help fix this, even if it meant going into the belly of the beast and visiting Rodge on his home turf. It was the only way.

Chapter 9

———————

I T WAS A long week, made longer by the amount of work I had on my plate, and the emotional upheaval threatening me. Hunter had his usual million projects going on, but Bruce had stepped up his production and requested a bunch more from me as well. I'd get home after a long day and walk straight into my office, starting the hobby job that didn't actually pay anything.

And then there was the contract.

I could see the stress eating away at Hunter every day. At work, I'd hear him shout into the phone, something I'd never heard him do before. When I took him his coffee, he might be pacing in front of the window. He tossed and turned at night. Occasionally, when he was in the middle of a nightmare, he'd mutter something along the lines of, "No, Dad, don't take this one!"

He was reliving his horror of the maid, the woman who ruined him before he'd even turned eighteen. The woman who'd chosen his dad over him, crushing his young, inexperienced heart. Hunter was applying that pain to me. He worried he'd lose me the same way.

On Friday, the day before I planned to take matters into my own hands, I called Kimberly, to ask her advice.

"Have you talked to him about the situation?" she asked.

"Yes. Well...I tried," I said as I paced my office. "He doesn't want to talk about it. Brenda said he's liquidizing a bunch of his assets, prepared to hand it over. This will devastate him, Kimberly. It might even bankrupt him."

"It won't bankrupt him, Livy. Not even close. The man has way too much money for that. Plus, he is so smart, he'll make it all back in no time. Don't worry about that. But he will have to start over on some things. All because of you."

I leaned against the wall. "I should feel blissful and happy that he likes me this much, but all I feel is guilt."

"He hasn't said he loved you, but he's prepared to lose practically everything for you..."

I could hear the excitement in her voice. She was missing the point here. "Kimberly, this isn't a romantic situation. I can't do this to him."

Kimberly scoffed in exasperation. "Olivia, he's making a choice. He could just marry Blaire, stay with her in a sham marriage for however long, like he'd originally planned, and then get an annulment. Who cares— certainly no one else would. That setup isn't unheard of. The fact that he won't do that and keep you as a mistress..."

I gripped the phone in anger, hating Kimberly's

squeals of delight. I put my hand to my head. I felt sick. "I have to fix this."

"Do *not* tell me you're going to go through with your dumb plan."

I wandered through the empty flat, which was huge and lonely. Hunter was staying at his place tonight, having said he would be working late. I thought he just wanted some time alone. Or maybe he intended to have it out with Blaire again. He had a lot at stake. I didn't begrudge him taking some time to reflect.

I just wished that didn't make me have to reflect too.

I plopped onto the couch and leaned back, closing my eyes. "I have to. It's the only way. He's trying to sacrifice for me, and what am I doing?"

"You're giving him what no one else can—a loving woman who isn't after his money."

"I'm giving him a headache at the same time as bleeding him dry." I shook my head. "I have to go."

"Well, then, I'm going with you," Kimberley said firmly.

"No, you're not." I rubbed my eyes, feeling tired and strung out.

"Olivia, if Hunter finds out you went to his father's house, he'll never trust you again, especially if you go alone. And if it works? He'll totally think you had sex with his dad. You don't want that. *He* doesn't want that. You need a witness."

"If you come with me, Rodge will know it's precisely because I needed a witness. I doubt he would bend if it wouldn't hurt Hunter in some way."

Kimberly was silent for a moment. "True. *Dang!* Wait...I've got it. We can do both—send you alone, and give you a witness."

"How? You have a crystal ball that works?"

I listened to her plan, feeling a fraction of relief work into my gloomy outlook. Her plan was a good one.

THE NEXT DAY, after I'd finished sorting out some things for Hunter and equally as much for Bruce, I slipped into a sexy, revealing dress and applied the brooch Kimberly had bought for me. The sun was just dipping behind the horizon as I walked out to the living room.

Kimberly and Janelle waited for me on the couch, their chatter dying down as I walked into their midst. Kimberly held up her phone, recording the situation on video.

"Okay, describe what you are wearing," Kimberly prompted.

I took a deep breath and put out my hands. "A sexy dress that Rodge will think I am wearing to try to seduce him."

"What else?" she continued.

I pointed to the brooch. "A spy brooch. This has a small camera in it that should catch most video, and will definitely catch the audio."

"Hopefully." Kimberly turned the phone so the camera was facing her. The screen pointed at me. "We tested—"

"Kimberly, all it sees is your chin. Turn the camera around." I adjusted the brooch, letting my hands fall away as Janelle got up and came over. She took over adjusting so it looked right.

"Oh." Kimberly rolled her eyes. "I'm stupid." She turned the phone back around before tapping the screen. She pushed the phone away a little, no doubt making sure to capture herself just right, and started again. "We tested it, and it seems to get fisheye kind of video and pretty good audio. If Livy doesn't go swimming with it, it should do the trick."

"I feel like a rinky-dink spy," I muttered, smoothing my dress.

Kimberly hit the screen again. "Tell him what else you have."

I looked around, holding my hand out for Janelle to give me my clutch. From it I took a small vial with a couple pills. "The secret weapon." I shook the vial, rattling the pills inside. "This will knock him out."

"What else?"

I groaned and took out a condom and a small bottle of lotion. I held them both up with a grimace. "The condom will be thrown on the ground. There is no way I am going to touch his penis."

"She is going to drug him, then she'll open his fly and shirt, so he thinks he got kinda naked. Then she'll leave the condom with lotion on the ground so he thinks he...you know."

"Ejaculated," Janelle added, tucking the items back

into my clutch with a grimace to match mine.

"Yeah. Gross. Then she'll leave." Kimberly brushed back her hair. The phone jiggled in her hand. I was pretty positive this video shoot wouldn't produce the best-quality picture.

"I will try to talk him into breaking the contract before I have to actually pretend to give it up, though," I explained, putting my wrap over my shoulders.

"No way will he pass up a chance to get you naked," Kimberly said in disgust. "That man is gross. And there's no way he will keep all this quiet. Which is why the video is essential."

"Right. As is the counter-contract we had drawn up." I took a piece of paper from the table.

"I don't think that's what it's called," Janelle said in her soft voice.

Kimberly tapped the screen and adjusted the phone again, now recording herself. "I explained everything to my lawyer and got him a copy of the contract you signed, Hunter. Don't ask me how—I'm sneaky. Anyway, he drew up something that will negate the contract if your dad signs it. Olivia, sacrificing herself, plans to subject herself to your gross dad in order to try and help you out and prove she loves you."

"Kimberly!" I screeched, clattering over in high heels to try and snatch the phone.

Kimberly gave an evil grin. "Not love, Hunter. Just...intense lust boardering on desperation to continue being with you—"

"Kim—berly!" I ripped the phone away and ended the recording. I glared down at her. "You better edit that out if you ever have to send this to him!"

"Livy, he *has* to know by now. You might as well just say it."

"One thing at a time. First, I need to get through tonight without damning myself. If I do have to drug this guy, he could rat me out. I'd go to jail."

"That's why you have to wait until the drug leaves his system before you come forward with the video."

"Except the video will show me slipping him the pills."

"Not if we edit the video, dummy." Kimberly winked at me. "I swear, you are terrible at espionage."

"Just make sure you provide plenty of evidence of him drinking heavily," Janelle said, fixing my hair. "That'll explain him passing out."

I took another deep breath, butterflies waging war in my stomach. I was no good at lying, and I hadn't forgotten how I had felt when Rodge had pushed himself on me.

I checked my clutch, running my fingers along the tiny bottle of pepper spray, just in case.

"I just hope Hunter forgives me for this if he finds out," I murmured as I placed the order for the cab. I didn't want to take a car in case Hunter got a report about who was taken where. My hope was that he'd never find out about this.

"We'll have proof nothing happened, Livy," Kimberly said. "We'll make sure he can't blame you."

I nodded miserably. "He wouldn't want me going at all. He'll be mad I took this upon myself."

"He'll get over it." Kimberly patted the couch. "Come sit down and have a glass of wine to relax."

"Janelle, you can go at any time," I said, moving toward Kimberly and the bottle of wine resting on the coffee table.

"I'll wait until you're tucked into the cab." She moved to sit down as well.

I took a sip of my wine with a shaky grip. I wasn't sure I was up to this.

AN HOUR LATER, I arrived at a large house in the East Bay. The immaculately landscaped front had a path cutting through it, dotted with ankle-high lights leading up to a grand front door surrounded by pillars. The porch light was on, as were various lights inside the house.

I sucked in a breath through a tight chest as I paid the cab driver. Climbing out of the car, I squeezed my clutch to my stomach, going over the various items inside. My brain constantly went back to the pepper spray.

I rang the doorbell with a shaking hand as the cab driver sped away.

Whatever happened to waiting to make sure the patron was safely inside...

Although, in this situation, that might have been

worse.

The door opened slowly. A young, pretty girl stood in front of me with large, luminous eyes and a heart-shaped mouth. She wore something like a French maid's outfit, with a white apron overlaying a little black dress. The hem of the skirt portion came to her mid-thigh, revealing long legs encased in fishnet stockings. Her ample cleavage peeked out of her low-cut top.

I could barely prevent myself from shaking my head in disgust. She was probably no more than eighteen, and wearing a revealing outfit designed to show off for her employer. Based on what I knew of Rodge's past, he not only looked, he sampled the merchandise. Disgusting.

"Miss Jonston?" the young woman asked in a sultry voice.

"Yes." I took a step forward.

"Follow me." She stepped to the side so that I might enter the house before closing the door behind me. She took her position as my guide, walking on high heels that couldn't possibly be comfortable to wear for the whole day, and swinging her generous hips.

We walked through the hallway, past the stairs leading to the upper floor, and into a dimly lit den. Books lined the wall and couches took up the middle of the floor, facing each other. Soft music played in the background as candles sent flickering light up around the room.

"Olivia." Rodge put down a snifter filled with an amber liquid before standing. His eyes glittered with arousal as a slow smile soaked up his features. "I'm so glad you could come."

"Hi, Rodge," I said, fighting to match his smile. It wasn't easy. The man gave me the creeps.

"Stacy, honey, will you bring in the trays?" Rodge didn't take his eyes from me as he spoke.

"Of course, Rod—Mr. Carlisle." She curtsied, of all things, and bustled out of the room.

"A little young, hmm?" I asked as I took a seat across from him on the couch.

He sat back down slowly, his eyes roaming my body. "She has no complaints."

"I bet not. I'm sure the money's good. And whatever happened to…your girlfriend?"

He smiled without humor as the maid returned, carrying a tray laden with finger foods. "Would you care for something to drink?" she asked.

"A red wine would be great, thanks."

"Stacy, honey…"

"Yes, sir, Mr. Carlisle." She walked to the left, where a small bar was stationed. From the countertop she took a bottle, inspected the label, and then opened it. She poured two glasses.

"Are you worried I might spike your drink, Livy?"

Cold trickled down my spine with the familiar way he spoke to me. I hated that he'd used my nickname. He held the power here, or at least he thought he did, and it showed in his tone. He saw this as a victory over me, and over his son.

I composed my face, doing everything I could not to grit my teeth or grimace. "A little," I replied honestly. "You're the type of man who is not afraid to cheat to get what he wants."

"Yes. I am." He gave me that slimy smile as he took his glass of wine from Stacy. He waited until I took mine before raising his a little in a silent salute. After he took a sip, he crossed a leg over his knee and got comfortable. "I've backed my son into a corner. He has no choice but to part with you for a night. You see, he's never been without more than enough money. Even though he'd be left with plenty of fortune for a normal man, he wouldn't know how to function. He hasn't had to scrape the bottom like I have. Add that to his lack of interest in those around him, and he'll give his prize to his sworn enemy."

"You have him all figured out."

"He's my son, after all." Rodge took a slow sip of his wine, watching me over the rim of his glass. "And once I've had you, he won't want you anymore. You do know that, right?"

I swallowed. I did know that. Even though I wouldn't sleep with Rodge, me being here would be enough to signify my guilt to Hunter. He'd be hard-pressed to believe me when I said I didn't touch his dad, and worse, he would have a hard time forgiving me, if he ever did. In Hunter's eyes, all this would be betraying him, not saving him. Hopefully the video would lessen the sting.

I took a sip, trying to hide my hand shaking. Rodge gave me that slow smile again.

"I knew Hunter would give you up, but I must admit, I didn't know if you would agree. You must really care for my son…"

"And by saying that, you're saying I must really *not* like you…"

Rodge chuckled as he reached to the table for a piece of cheese, bringing his body closer to me. "Part of this is exciting because I will be conquering you, of course."

"And that doesn't bother your ego at all, huh? Having to coerce a woman into bed?"

"Not at all. Some women flock to me because of money, some power—women always want something."

"What a limited view you have of the female species. So, by your definition, I am after something. What is that?"

Rodge's eyes shone as he looked at me. "My son, of course."

"Yes, but it's an act of selflessness. That's not wanting something—that's giving to make someone else happy. I don't fit into your definition of a female."

"If I allow him to get out of this contract, he'll also have more money than me. More power. You're going for the big prize."

"Except when he finds out I'm here, he won't want me. So what's the prize?"

Rodge popped the cheese into his mouth as he stared at me. His eyes marginally squinted. "That, I'm afraid, I haven't figured out. You're a smart girl—much smarter than the girls he usually employs. What *is* your angle, Livy? You must have one."

Stacy walked in. "Sir, dinner is ready."

I stood, hardly having taken a sip of my wine. Rodge stood with me, still staring. Trying to figure me out.

I gave him a sly smile. "Like I said, I don't fit into your definition of female."

"You do. I just have to find out how."

I rolled my eyes as I followed Stacy. We passed through spacious rooms decorated with dark colors and strange modern art. The smell of cooking wafted toward me as we passed through an archway to a room with a large dining table featuring a large but low arrangement of flowers. The lights were dim here too. Two place settings faced each other across the middle of the table. I had hoped we would each be at either end, but he'd gone for the intimate approach. Unfortunately.

I sat where Stacy indicated, putting my glass in front of me and resting my clutch on my knees, hidden by the tablecloth. My goal was to slip the drug into his drink toward the end of dinner, so that when we moved to a more intimate setting, he was already feeling drowsy.

How I would do that was a concern. A big one. I wasn't very sneaky.

"You just want to get the night over with," Rodge said as he settled.

My stomach turned. Knowing my expression probably showed my distaste, I took a sip of wine. Lowering it slowly, I cleared my throat. "I'm here to fulfill my end of the agreement. I don't have to like it, and, quite frankly, don't plan to. But I'm no fool, Rodge. I don't intend to…go through with this unless I have something signed from you, waiving your rights."

"What would you have me do, scribble it on a napkin?" He laughed as Stacy and another pretty girl, about the same age, and wearing the same outfit, delivered soup.

"I brought something for you to sign. I won't touch you until it's signed." I waited until the soup was in front of me and the women gone before I picked up my spoon and swirled it around. I had no appetite, and I really wondered if there was something in the food. I planned to drug him and leave—I wouldn't put it past him to do the same to keep me here.

Rodge's face lost the smile. His eyes turned shrewd. "I'll sign it after."

"No way. I want it before, or I'll leave right now. I don't trust you."

Rodge lifted the spoon to his mouth and sipped his soup slowly, some sort of creamy concoction that actually smelled really great.

"Why do you want me, really, Rodge?" I asked despite myself. "You can get younger, obviously. And prettier. Why waste your time trying to force me? Why do you hate your son that much?"

"I don't hate my son. But I don't like that he's trying to rise above his station. I *made* him. I taught him, gave him a place to start his career. What does he do? He takes what I offer, and then uses it to leverage a better position. It doesn't stop there. Rather than waiting until I die to receive his inheritance, he works out a deal to cut me out of his life early. Now I don't have as much to offer another heir that *would* follow my teaching. So you see, I'm just balancing out the power once again. That's all."

"What's the matter, can't marry into money again? All the women with their own fortunes see you coming, and the young ones still have Daddy to protect them?"

He sneered at me. "I wouldn't expect you to understand my situation."

"That's probably a compliment." I moved my spoon around my soup. "So you're restacking the power in your favor…"

Rodge gave me a smug smile. "Exactly. As it should be with father and son."

"You don't have any other kids, though."

"No." Rodge's eyes flicked down at his soup for a brief moment as a sour expression crossed his face. It was gone almost immediately.

"Ah. Not for lack of trying, though. You think going young will help, but it's the old sperm that's the problem…"

His eyes snapped up to me, anger blasting out. Just like his expression from a moment before, though, the emotion was gone a moment later. Back to cool and collected, but I had affected him. That was a sore subject.

"Anyway," I said, "you'll have me, you'll devastate him again—so you think—and then you will, what? Dance naked in the moonlight? What will you gain?"

Rodge gave a small shrug. "The upper hand. With a man like Hunter, the upper hand is a great thing. It really gets under his skin."

"You sound like an adolescent." The girls came and removed our soup. I saw that Rodge's was nearly empty, and I got a quirked eyebrow from Stacy, as my bowl was still almost full.

Next came a chicken dish that also smelled truly divine. This I did sample, though with a churning stomach from just being in Rodge's presence, not to mention the fear of what Hunter would say if he found out. I didn't eat much before I laid down my fork and knife.

"So tell me," Rodge said conversationally as he cut into his meat, "how do you like graduating from a pristine college with a great education, only to become a secretary?"

"First, executive assistants for large corporations make a lot of money. Second, I do much more than administrative duties."

"Of course you do." He gave me a condescending smile as he raised his fork to his mouth. "And what will you do when Hunter fires you for fucking his father?"

With shaking hands, I pushed my plate away and put my hands on my clutch. I took out the vial and emptied one of the pills into my palm. I had no idea how I was going to get it into his glass, but it was better to be ready than miss an opportunity.

"I guess I'll just have to wait and see…" I said in the same conversational tone.

Rodge laughed, putting another bite into his mouth. "I'm no longer hiring, if that was your thought."

"It wasn't."

"I also don't have room for a mistress."

"I'm heartbroken."

Rodge took a sip of his wine. "You seem like such a soft touch, Olivia. I thought you'd be a doormat. But you have some fire to you. You know your own mind."

"And let me guess—you hate that in a woman."

He laughed again, putting down his cutlery. "Only when she says no."

The girls came out and removed the plates. I got another quirked eyebrow. Dessert came and went, and eventually he stood, gesturing for me to do the same.

"Shall we move to the den, Livy?"

My stomach swirled and twisted. I followed him with shaking limbs and the overwhelming impulse to cry. I felt trapped. I wanted Hunter to come and save me, as stupid as that was. I wanted him to just barge in, say he'd found another way, and let me run out of here.

I followed behind Rodge, and sat on the couch where I'd been before. This time, he sat right next to me. His cologne assaulted my nose and stung my eyes, the fragrance probably delightful on someone else, but sickly sweet on him.

"I need you to sign that waiver," I said with a trembling voice I couldn't help. I scooted a little away, hating that his thigh was rubbing against mine.

"What's to prevent you from leaving if I sign it?"

Rodge's voice was low and husky. I felt a finger run softly up my arm.

Shivering in disgust, I bent forward to my clutch, the pill still in my hand. I took out the folded waiver and held it up to him. "I'll let you keep hold of it until after, and then I'll take it and go. Immediately. I'm not sleeping in the same bed as you."

Rodge took the piece of paper from me. He leaned forward and put his glass on the coffee table before straightening back up, angling away from me to catch some light in which to read.

Seeing my opportunity, I grabbed the open bottle of wine left from before and poured us both full glasses. As I turned to straighten back up, I glanced at him, seeing him struggling to read the print. I dropped the pill into his drink, laughing to cover the small *plunk*. "Need glasses?" I taunted.

Rodge's brows lowered as his eyes shifted back and forth over the page.

"You had someone draw this up," he said.

"Obviously. I'm not an idiot."

He lowered the paper, looking at me with a shrewd gaze. "Why are you doing this? I have to know."

"I'm the reason Hunter is in this mess. I'll be the reason he gets out. I owe him that much."

Rodge squinted. "Why else? You don't owe him your dignity."

I sipped my wine, remembering Kimberly's comment about editing. "I love him."

Rodge laughed heartily at that, putting the waiver down on the table and taking up his wine glass. He took a large sip before shaking his head. "Now I see. Ensnared. You think this will make him love you back. What a fool you are. You should be after the money or power." He shook his head again. "My son doesn't love, Olivia. You must know that. He won't get soft-hearted because you risked yourself for him."

"I don't plan to tell him. I'd hoped you'd do the right thing and let me go..."

He stood smoothly and crossed the room to a small desk in the corner. From it he extracted a pen, his eyes sparkling in the firelight when he was on his way back. When he returned, he casually signed and dated the form, leaving it where it was when he was through. He tossed the pen across the coffee table, took another sip of wine, and twisted toward me from the edge of the couch. His gaze roamed my body.

"No. But if you're good, and you scream real nice, I won't tell him. You have to let yourself thoroughly enjoy it, though. I'm not the man you think, Livy. My hands can be surprisingly gentle..."

I tried to swallow past the lump in my throat. I knew he was being crude just to make this worse for me. He was playing mind games. I also knew he would try to get me to enjoy it so I hated myself for it. He'd take more time with that goal in mind.

I had no intention of being around that long.

Chapter 10

I TOOK UP my glass of wine and eyed the bottle. "Do I have to be sober for this?"

He smiled as I took a big gulp of my wine. He followed suit, drinking most before setting his glass down and waiting for me.

"Seriously. More." I held out my glass. Smirking, he filled it, and filled his as well, emptying the bottle.

"Why Blaire?" I asked, allowing him to hear the tremor in my voice. I wanted him to think I was stalling because I was nervous. Which I was.

He leaned back with his body facing me. He strung his arm across the top of the couch, bending at the elbow so he could flick my hair with his fingers. "Her father had a struggling business when the economy crippled him. I wanted in on it, so I offered a bailout. Little did I know my shares wouldn't be worth much when all was said and done."

"Why didn't you marry her yourself?"

"And take something her father wanted to get rid of?

The woman is wild. She's a handful, and she spends like the spoiled brat she is. I wanted nothing to do with her."

His fingers trailed down my cheek.

I shivered, but prevented myself from jerking away. His oily smile said I didn't prevent the grimace, though.

"So you pawned her off on your son."

"Yes I did. I figured he'd just get used to her and eventually try to get her knocked up so he could finally have a child." His delighted smile set off warning bells.

"And why does that amuse you?" I asked in a weak voice, trying to ignore his hand trailing down my neck.

"Because she can't have babies. Or so her father said when he'd had too much brandy. She got her tubes tied—never wanted the little leeches, apparently."

"And Hunter doesn't know that?"

"Of course not."

I blinked in disbelief. "Are you a sociopath? You're his *father*! How can you be so cruel?"

"Like I said, *he* left *me.* My company wasn't good enough for him. Too small. I don't let betrayal go unpunished."

I rolled my eyes, and then shuddered in disgust as his hand dipped in toward my chest and ran over the swell of my breast.

"I can't—" I jerked away, hating his touch. Hating this house and everything about this.

I squeezed my eyes tight, desperately wondering why I hadn't used two pills. "I need to use the bathroom."

"Stalling just prolongs the inevitable," he said with a

smile in his voice.

I opened my eyes, my hate-filled glare landing on him. It made his smile burn brighter. I looked at the waiver lying on the table.

"I'll do you right near, then you can take it and go. No sassle."

The lump in my throat was back. My eyes stung. I hated this. Only then did what he had said leak into my brain.

I turned back to him, noticing his eyes drooping just a little bit. Swallowing, I leaned back, aiming my chest toward him so the camera would catch everything. I didn't make a move toward him, though. I left my hands in my lap, stiff.

His smile turned hungry. He reached out with a slightly limp hand, hitting the center of my chest. His brow creased a little as he adjusted, flopping his palm onto my breast.

"Just get this over with," I said, turning my face toward the couch back.

As expected, he chuckled darkly, slowing down. He moved over to the other breast before working with numb fingers at the strap on my dress.

"Snur faburn." His eyebrows pinched over his eyes before his head rolled. He looked at his hand before his head rolled again. His body fell against the couch back, and he reached out to me.

I caught his hand by the wrist and held it. He pulled back, which only succeeded in tipping his body toward me when I wouldn't let go of his hand. I hopped up quickly, grabbed his glass, crossed the room to the small bar, and poured it down the sink. I did the same with mine, then brought the decanter of brandy to the coffee table and left it there, along with two snifter glasses, both with a little of the brown liquid in the bottom.

Moving quickly, I took out the condom and lotion before snatching the waiver from the coffee table and jamming it into my clutch. With shaking hands, hoping none of the maids tiptoed in to check on things, I made sex sounds as I ripped the condom pack and unrolled the latex. I squeezed the small bit of white lotion into the end before dropping it and the wrapper on the ground.

A quick glance told me the coast was still clear, so I heaved his body fully onto the couch, on his back, before ripping open his fly and yanking it down.

"This so sucks," I muttered, ripping his shirt open. Buttons flew all over. I didn't care. I yanked open his pants a moment later and reached into his small briefs to find an erect penis.

"Oh, ew," I said with bile rising in my throat. He must've taken Viagra.

Gagging, skin crawling, I put some of the lotion onto him, just to make it seem used a little, and wiped my hands on his pants. I put the unused lotion into my clutch, so no one would be the wiser, and grunted sexually a few times in a male voice.

There was no way this would fool anyone, but I had to try.

Straightening up, and mussing my hair and clothes, I quickly swept my gaze around the area to make sure everything was in order, took off my shoes so I didn't make too much noise, and snuck off toward the door. Hopefully no one would check on him for a while.

I left the house and slipped on my shoes, bringing out my phone to call a cab. As I hurried down the front walk, I caught sight of someone walking in rapid strides toward me. My breath caught as I lowered the phone, ready to run or scream or who knew what.

"Olivia."

The dominating voice shocked into me, releasing the stress from my body and relaxing my muscles. I should've been nervous as Hunter reached me and grabbed my shoulders. I was on enemy soil, after all. But I wasn't. Not even a little. Just utterly, completely relieved.

"What happened? Are you okay?" he asked.

His gaze went to my hair and then down to my clothes, lingering on the brooch for a second. He looked back at my eyes. "Did he touch you?"

Tears of relief came to my eyes. "No. He didn't do anything. I'm okay."

Hunter pulled me in, squeezing me tightly to his chest.

"What are you doing here?" I asked in a breathy voice, not able to properly breathe with his bear hug, and not caring.

"First, I need to sort this out—" Hunter released me

and turned toward the street. "My car is over there. It's unlocked. Get in and wait for me there."

"No!" I stepped into the middle of the path hastily, putting my hands out. "You can't go in there!"

His expression closed down into one of suspicion. "Why?"

I took the vial and the waiver out of my clutch and held it up to Hunter. "One, because I drugged him, which is illegal. Two, because I got what I came for. This absolves your contract. Or...absolves Rodge's portion—I'm not really sure how it works. But Kimberly's lawyer drew it up, so it's binding. All you have to do is file it and you should be okay."

Hunter took the waiver slowly, scanning the writing before glancing at the moon. He must not have had enough light to see what it said. He took the vial next, wiggling the little bottle. The remaining pill clattered against the plastic. His gaze hit me again. "How did you get him to sign this without—"

"Can I explain in the car, please? I have no idea when his maids will check on him. I'd rather not get caught out here."

Hunter glanced at the door again, his expression turning into a mask of cold anger. The small hairs on my neck rose as his upper body muscles flexed against his shirt. He wanted to go in and have words with his father.

His chest rose before he exhaled loudly. He brushed the stray hairs from my face before sliding his arm around my shoulder and leading me back to his car parked across the street.

Once on the road, I asked again, "What were you doing there?"

"I came home—excuse me. I showed up at your flat after I took care of some things. Kimberly and Janelle were there watching the remote transmission from your brooch. They didn't think I'd be over…"

"I didn't either. Earlier today you didn't think you would…"

"Two nights without you is too many."

Shivers raced across my arms. I couldn't help the delighted smile, masked by the darkness in the car.

"You were just sitting down to dinner. I…wasn't happy when I realized where you were." His voice dropped in pitch, the anger at the discovery burning hot. "Kimberly tried to explain, but I was already headed for the door. She played the video as she chased me to the car. What was being said finally sank in as I was sitting into the seat. I watched the whole thing then. Listening to you two explaining what you were doing. She told me why…"

"I couldn't let you lose everything for me."

His hand balled into a fist in his lap. "My father isn't the most trustworthy person. What if you'd got yourself in too deep and couldn't get away?"

I reached into my clutch and pulled out the pepper spray. "Then I would've sprayed him."

Hunter rolled his shoulders, getting onto the on ramp to cross the Bay Bridge. "I wish you hadn't done that. This. Any of this. This shouldn't concern you."

"But it does. You wouldn't be in this mess if it wasn't for me. Also, did you know that Blaire can't have kids? She doesn't want them."

"Yes. I do. She threw that in my face at one point. It wouldn't have mattered. She was a means to an end. She wasn't any more cruel than I was. We each wanted certain things. I'm the one that backed out. She deserved more."

I scoffed. "Yeah, right. She was in it for the money."

"So was I."

"No harm, no foul, then. Plus, you can't tell me you were *just* in it for the money. You were also preventing your father from siring another heir, weren't you? He took a bunch from your mom that wasn't his, and if he'd had another kid, he would've split the inheritance. Or cut you out entirely."

Hunter's jaw tightened, the green from the dash illuminating his handsome features. "You must've had a long chat with my father."

I laughed. "I might've...goaded him a little. He's just so creepy. And *such* an asshole. I would advise you not to watch the transmission." I glanced out the window, wiping under my eyes to clear any straying makeup. "He spelled out why he's such an ass to you. Basically, he thinks you betrayed him. That's all you really need to know."

"I did know that. He's not as sly as he thinks he is. He wanted to sit on his empire with his son pulling strings and helping him with his unethical tricks. Since I wouldn't, I became the enemy."

"And I thought my mom was bad…"

"Can't even compare. Your mother is narcissistic. My father is…"

"Evil."

Hunter kept his silence for a while. The rumble of the car filled the space as the streetlights flashed by. The scenes from the night flashed by with them, my memory highlighting all the things that could've gone wrong. All the things that almost did go wrong. I got lucky. Barely, but I did get lucky.

"Are you mad?" I asked in a whisper. "That I went to his house, I mean. Are you fighting trust issues or anything?"

He glanced over before moving his right hand off the steering wheel and taking mine. "No. I'm not mad. Or suspicious. I can't say I wouldn't have been, though. If you hadn't recorded it, and if Kimberly hadn't explained… You know me. Better than anyone else. You can read me."

"It's not hard. A person just has to pay attention."

"Not many would. Or do." His fingers threaded in between mine. "I was afraid that I'd be too late. That something would happen and you wouldn't be able to get away. I underestimated you."

I scoffed, still staring out the window. "That's not hard. Even Kimberly said I was terrible at espionage. You should also know that I had to touch his…you know. It was gross, but it had to be believable. I don't want to go to jail."

"You won't." His voice filled with power and determination. "Nothing from tonight will come near you. I'm sorry that you thought it did in the first place."

I dropped my head against the seat as he said, "So you followed through with your plan. With the condom and…"

"Yeah. That's why I had to touch…you know."

"And he signed on his own? You didn't forge?"

"He signed. I said I wouldn't touch him unless he signed. He thought I would go through with it at that point. If I hadn't drugged him, I wouldn't have been able to take the waiver unless he let me. He thought he was in control."

Hunter nodded slowly as he pulled into the garage of my flat. When the car was silent, he sat for a moment, holding my hand without moving. Finally, he looked over at me, the light from the garage shining in and highlighting his features. "Thank you, for what you did. It was an act of selflessness. I realize that. Regardless of my hang-ups over your involvement…thank you."

"I was worried you'd find out and not understand."

"I know," he whispered. He leaned over and touched his lips to mine softly. "I don't deserve a woman like you. I haven't done anything in my life to warrant this luck."

"You're calling hanging out with me luck? I'd better get that engraved—no one will believe you actually said *luck*. As opposed to misery."

He kissed me again, deeper this time. Warmth filled my body, my mind falling into the kiss as I had into his eyes a few moments ago.

"C'mon," he murmured against my lips. "Let's go upstairs."

Something occurred to me as we walked up the stairs and into the flat. He dropped his keys into the bowl by the door and led me down the hall to our—my—room. "You watched the whole video Kimberly took?"

He switched on the light and turned to me, pulling me into his body. His lips found my neck, kissing down to my collarbone. "Yes."

"The *whole* video?"

"Yes." He pushed my hair from my face as he kissed my jaw, and then my lips. His hands fell down to my shoulders, pushing the dress straps down my arms. The dress slunk down my chest and then thighs before pooling on the floor.

"There was talk of editing things out…"

My bra fell away. His hot tongue flicked my taut nipple, sending shooting sparks of pleasure throughout my body. His hands skimmed my ribs. Thumbs hooked into the elastic of my panties where they wrapped around my waist. He pushed the lacy material down.

"Yes," he said right before his hot mouth fastened around the nipple, sucking.

My head fell back as deft fingers worked between my slit, making everything slick. Two fingers pushed into me as his thumb circled my clit. "And me trying to get the video away from her..."

His mouth left a trail of heat up to my lips. He shrugged out of his dress shirt before unbuttoning and pushing down his pants and boxers. He pulled me closer again, the feel of his delicious body against mine making my eyes flutter closed.

"Yes." He kissed me passionately, his hands applying pressure on my back until my front was basically coating his. He shifted a little, backing away to adjust. His erection slid between my legs, rubbing against my incredibly wet and aching sex.

I sighed as his lips sucked softly at my neck. His hands rubbed down my bare back and squeezed my butt cheeks. His hips moved away and then came back, rubbing his soft skin against mine.

"And you're not going to fire me for breaking the rules?" I asked in a hush, torn between extremely turned on, and uncomfortable because I knew he'd heard the love admission.

"We've broken a lot of rules, Livy." Hunter sighed as he pulled his hips away, dragging his velvety manhood against me. He angled up and brought his hips back in. His tip pushed past my barriers and entered my body slowly, filling me up.

I slid a leg up his thigh and hooked it around his hip. He nibbled my lips as he pulled out, rubbing just right. He thrust slowly, deep and intense. His tongue entered my mouth, matching his body's movements. He pulled out, and this time, his thrust came hard and fast.

The contrast made me moan, melting into him in erotic bliss.

"I want to pleasure you, Livy." Hunter pulled out of me. "Pull the sheets back. Get your heating lotion, the handcuffs, and the blindfold."

Chapter 11

A THRILL ZINGED through my body. With tingling legs and a nervous smile, I went to the closet and retrieved what he'd asked for. When I came back, he took the items from me before turning me around. The soft material covered my eyes, tightening as he tied it behind my head. I felt the whisper of fingertips down my arms, giving me goosebumps.

His heat moved away, leaving my back uncomfortably cold. In darkness, I heard the bed creak and shift, fabric being ruffled. Metal jingled. Butterflies filled my stomach.

I'd never done this before. I'd never trusted someone enough to let them tie me down in any way. I'd never met someone that I could trust so completely.

I'd also never been with someone like Hunter.

Without warning, he scooped me up into his arms. I squealed in surprise. A moment later, I felt his muscles lengthen and contract around me, as he climbed onto the bed. The soft mattress received me as he put me down.

He drew up my hands above my head. Cold metal encircled each wrist.

Another thrill tore through me as the ratchet sound announced the handcuffs closing. I moved, feeling the shackles catch and hold my wrists.

A warm hand settled on my shin before moving up my body slowly. It traveled over my thigh, going wide around my hip and over my belly. I sucked in a breath as his palm cupped a breast. His thumb ran across my nipple.

I moaned, arching into his hand. His other hand touched down on my other breast, his thumbs now moving and tweaking both nipples.

I licked my lips and spread my legs, pulling at my hands, feeling the fire of being completely at his mercy. His hands left my breasts, making me whimper in disappointment. A moment later, though, cool wetness rubbed into my breasts and around my nipples. Between my legs was next. My nipples began to tingle with heat before my sex did the same, the warming lotion spiking the pleasure.

The bed moved under me. Some part of him glanced across my thigh. The soft *clunk* of the lotion bottle touched down on the nightstand. I felt his movement before a warm tongue licked up my center.

"Oh," I moaned, tilting up into him. Palms pushed my thighs wider. His mouth sucked me in, his tongue swirling as it did so. His palms disappeared. I waited, wondering where they would touch down as his mouth moved up. His tongue played with my clit, his hands still absent.

I breathed out the expectation. My core started to tighten in excitement as I gyrated up into him. I pulled at my hands, deliciously trapped. I arched, moaning as his suction increased.

A finger flicked my nipple unexpectedly.

"Oh!" I jolted, throwing my head back into the pillow. I pulled at my hands again and bit my lip. His mouth worked me harder as his fingers gently twisted my nipple.

Shooting jabs of pleasure shocked into my body, pooling in my sex. The tightness intensified, winding up. I writhed, unable to move far with my hands caught. Unable to touch him.

"Yes, Hunter," I said through a tight throat, gyrating into his mouth. I strained against the handcuffs and arched, wanting his touch harder. Wanting more.

His hand rubbed down my stomach. Another hand joined the first, firm strokes down my lower belly and over my thighs. I spread my legs wider and arched again, needing his touch to work with his mouth. Needing a part of him inside me.

As if reading my mind, one of his hands lifted, appearing on my breast. The other felt down my slit before dipping in.

"Oh, yes. Oh. Yes!" Unable to help myself, so damn aroused by the cuffs and blindfold, at his mercy, I writhed on the bed wildly. I swung my hips into and away from him, working with the pounding of his fingers inside me. I felt the pull of his mouth on my most sensitive spot. Aching in my core from his other hand rubbing my breast.

I bit my lip again, pulling at the bed. Struggling. Wanting to touch him. Turned on that I couldn't.

"Yes, Hunter. Harder—" The sensations burned through me. My heart hammered as everything clenched tight deep down inside of me. So tight. Felt so *good*—

"*Ah!*" I shuddered uncontrollably in release, pulling with my hands. The wood cracked under the strain.

Hunter's hands roamed over me, softly sending waves of pleasant shivers through me. I panted, rubbing my thighs along his body as his soft breath blew against my fevered and aching sex.

"Fuck me now, Hunter," I commanded, somehow feeling more powerful even though I was tied up and blinded.

His body rubbed up mine, as my taut nipples rubbed against his harder pecs, ripping a moan from my throat. His lips hit mine. His tongue penetrated my mouth as my legs spread wider to accommodate his large body.

Without hesitation, he entered me, diving in deep. I moaned, wrapping my legs around his waist. His kiss deepened as he plunged, thrusting into me. Filling me up.

I started gyrating again, having skipped the second warmup phase and already tightening in anticipation of an orgasm. The bed shifted as he plunged, hard and fast.

The wood creaked with the strain of me pulling on it, loving being tied down. Loving being *taken*.

"Yes, Hunter!" I exalted. Our breath mingled, both of us breathing hard. I rocked my hips, meeting his downward thrusts. Our bodies slapped together. My moans grew louder.

"Olivia," Hunter whispered in my ear. He sucked in my earlobe as he dove into me.

Heat, then a slow burn, took over me. I wanted to admit I loved him. That I needed him.

I bit down on my lip. I held it in. Just in case. He knew, but he hadn't heard it straight from my lips.

Instead, I arched up, taking more of him. "Oh, Hunter. Oh God—I'm going to come." It hit me. Blistering pleasure exploded and then wrapped around me, so tight it cut off my breath. Colors blasted behind my eyes. I trembled beneath him, feeling him shaking over me.

His lips found mine again, deep and sensual. His movements slowed way down. "It just keeps getting better with you," he said softly, reaching up and undoing my blindfold. His handsome face and soft eyes came into view. Moonlight sprinkled across his shoulders.

He kissed me again as he let me out of the handcuffs.

"This bed was chosen specifically, wasn't it?" I asked with a tired smile, turning to my side. He pulled the covers over us and snuggled in behind me. "You wanted something you could use handcuffs with."

"Aren't you glad I did?"

I sighed in contentment as his arms came around me. "Yes. I liked that."

He kissed my neck. "So did I."

THE NEXT DAY I poked my head into the spare bedroom Hunter used as an office. He sat hunched over the desk with his hands clasped and his arms flexed.

"You okay?" I asked softly, only my head visible. He'd had an outburst a moment before, something he only did when dealing with the contract with Blaire.

He looked up and unclasped his hands. A smile adorned his face. "That waiver will hold up in court if my father takes it that far. Blaire's father had already backed out, and the small print was written with Blaire having absolutely no power of her own. It's resolved. I'm free of it."

Delight bubbled up through me. I stepped further into the room. "Are you relieved?"

"Very." He sighed. "It's amazing. It's like a weight has been lifted. I had no idea it had affected me this much. I have you to thank."

"Meh." I waved him away, leaning against the wall and crossing my arms. "Just call me private eye."

"For that, too, but I meant…for helping me see that there was more to life than a shallow contract and a stressful domestic setting."

"Stressful domestic setting? I don't think that does what you've been dealing with justice. I mean, finding strange, naked men on your coffee table must have traumatized you."

"Come here." He held out a hand. I took it and let him pull me onto his lap. He put his arms around my waist. "Nothing really traumatized me, no. But it was a constant nuisance. I didn't like going home."

"Again. Don't blame you. She's very pretty, but insane."

He gave me a squeeze. "My dad knows you drugged him. He says he's going to fight that waiver."

I froze in Hunter's arms. He gave me another squeeze. "He's not going to get proof for his suspicions. You have nothing to worry about."

I let out a sigh of relief. "But you said the waiver would hold up—how else would he fight it?"

"I told him you had a recording, both video and audio, of your dealings with him. He said a lot of things he wouldn't want anyone to hear last night. With that document in excellent shape, and his signature legit, he's got nothing. He can't even hold over me that he was with you—I told him about the lotion."

"Wait..." I turned so I could see Hunter's face. "How do you know what was said?"

"I watched the transmission. It's saved on your computer."

My mouth dropped open. It hadn't been edited. Rodge had signed the paper because I said I loved Hunter. Which, yes, was redundant to the other video, but this time I'd said it. It'd come out of my own mouth.

"I don't think it's healthy to sleep as much as you do." He winked and stood me up.

"But..." I blinked down at him. "You're not mad? Or weirded out about things...that were said..."

His eyes softened. "I'm not sure. And I'm battling some things that still haunt me from the past, but no. I won't fire you for breaking that rule."

The love rule, he meant. He was okay with me loving him.

The warmth that had been growing these past weeks flooded me. I'd dropped the L-bomb prematurely before. It hadn't worked out well.

I smiled like an idiot. I didn't even care that he had no plans to say it back yet. He was okay with it. The rest would come. "Okay, then."

"Remember, next Friday is the dinner party with my mother. Blaire is going to be there, so...we'll have that to deal with."

Hunter turned back to his laptop as if he hadn't dropped a huge bomb in the middle of this conversation.

"Blaire? At your mother's?"

"My mom sent the invite to my house with both of our names on it. She doesn't agree with my dealings with Blaire, but she's the type to ignore unpleasant things—it's how she coped with my father for so long."

"Does Blaire know you're definitely out of the contract?"

Hunter leaned against the desk again, bowing his head. His shoulders flexed in irritation. "Yes. I've given her a month to move out, and she's responded with a great many threats. She's going to turn up wherever I am. I have no idea who she'll bring to my mother's house, if anyone, but her sole focus will be me. She doesn't like losing."

"Is that who you were yelling at?"

"I don't yell, Livy. Although I do, occasionally, loudly state important facts."

"Ah." I smirked and made my way to my office, which was a storm of boxes. Janelle had done a great job bringing everything over from my old apartment. She'd even gotten help, she'd said. Jane had stayed out of the way or opened the door, always smiling pleasantly. Those months when I didn't have much money obviously strained her view of me, and she was another woman who could hold a grudge.

I pouted as I read the rooms of the house written on the side of the boxes. There were three total—bedroom, bathroom, and kitchen. The kitchen only had one box, and within it, two appliances. Or so the detailed description noted. I had a feeling the appliances were things Jane wanted to get rid of, because I didn't remember having anything.

I moved three bedroom boxes out of the way so I could get to the first bathroom one I'd seen. Tearing into it, I found soap and face wash and things I'd already bought to tide me over. I didn't find my three unopened packs of birth control pills.

Frowning, I looked for the next bathroom box.

"Why are they all on the bottom?" I asked in exasperation.

"What's that?"

I jumped and spun around. Hunter paused in the door with raised eyebrows.

"I was talking to myself. Butt out." I turned back to the stack of boxes.

"I was thinking of going out to dinner, and then stopping by my house and getting a few things. When can you be ready?"

I blew out a breath, blowing my hair away from my face. "Now, if you help me get these bathroom boxes out when we get back."

"Sure. Let's go."

"Pushy." I smiled and followed him into our—my—room.

I hadn't thought of this flat as being solely mine since I'd moved in, and neither had he. I wondered what would happen when Blaire finally moved out of his place. Would I stay with him again, or would he continue coming here when he wanted to see me?

The shower started. "Come in here, Livy. I need to fuck you."

All the thoughts fell out of my head. I'd have to revisit my desire to skip toward the bathroom. That couldn't be normal. "Yes, sir."

THE WEEK WENT by quickly. Hunter stayed over every night, setting off before me in the mornings, as usual, but often leaving the office with me. He worked out, ate, and finished up a few things from "my" building. Mrs. Foster now had a key to the flat and made breakfast for us, with Janelle doing the late shift and making dinner. Because of the shift changes and the two assistants combining efforts, Hunter and I got a fresh meal whenever we wanted it. Between them, they cleaned, straightened, and organized our whole lives.

I really loved my life. Money might not be able to buy happiness, but it could sure ease the troubles and promote laziness.

The only thing that was still going horribly wrong was Blaire. The woman would not let it rest. She'd found out where the flat was, and waited for Hunter a few days a week. Once she got face time, she was slinky and sexy and ready to seduce him at a moment's notice. She'd even reached for his zipper on the street like a crack-whore needing a fix and willing to do anything to get it. The whole situation was madness.

"You have that dinner tonight?" Brenda asked as I was packing my computer up.

I glanced at the clock. It was still only four, leaving me three hours to get ready. I'd probably need all three, too, because Blaire would be there, looking drop-dead gorgeous.

"Yeah." I slung the pack over my shoulder. "With the mother."

"She's a sweet lady," Brenda said, swiveling in her chair and facing me. "Mind your manners, though, because she's very…wealthy."

"Like, proper?"

Brenda gave one large head-bob. "Yes. Prim and proper at all times. It stresses me out."

"When did you meet her?"

"She's come through here a few times. Usually for Hunter's birthday. She'll take him to lunch or dinner."

I stepped into the doorway to Hunter's office. "I'm headed out."

He looked up from his computer, nodded, then turned back to his work. He didn't balk at the extra time it would take me to get ready. He knew the score.

"You're supposed to say goodbye…" I waited for a reaction. I saw his lips quirk upward, but he ignored me. He would start saying please, thank you, and goodbye, so help me God. He might even give me chocolates and flowers. Why not? If I was going to put the effort in, I might as well go big.

Just not today. I had to beautify.

"Okay. See you on the flip side," I said to Brenda as I passed.

"Yup. Have a good weekend."

Bert was waiting for me by the curb. It then took an hour to get home. Those seven miles were a killer. I really hated living so far away from the city center.

As we pulled up, Bert let out a low whistle. "That's not good."

I glanced up from my phone where I'd been looking at code. It took a second for my eyes to adjust. When they did, I saw what Bert was looking at. Scrawled across the garage in bright pink spray paint was the word "Bitch!"

"Great," I muttered, looking hard at the door. It was still closed, thank God. Hopefully that meant she hadn't been able to get into the house. I had no doubt that this had been done by Blaire. She was a sore loser.

"Do you want me to go in with you?" Bert asked.

"Yes, please," I said in a small voice. "It looks like Blaire wasn't thrilled Hunter got out of the contract."

Bert clicked on the hazards and got out of the car. He came around and opened my door before shadowing me through. The walls in the hallway looked fine, and the door to the flat itself was untouched.

"Here, Livy, let me." Bert took the keys from my shaking hand and opened the door. He stepped in first, the giant muscles on his body flexing. His huge arms drifted away from his sides, ready to fight.

I blinked at him for a moment. I'd never seen him get aggressive. He'd always been sweet around me. But as he walked into the kitchen with nimble feet, perfectly balanced, it was like seeing a complete stranger.

"What did you say you did before being Hunter's driver?" I asked with a dry mouth. I knew he would never hurt me, but truth be told, I worried about what he would do to whoever he found.

"I did a little boxing before playing in the NFL." He passed me by, having looped around through the living room, and was now headed toward the back of the flat.

"I think it's okay, Livy."

I stared after him. "The NFL? And you need a job?"

A moment later he walked toward me again, his body seemingly deflated and his happy-go-lucky outlook back in place. I wasn't fooled, though.

"It's clear." He smiled and handed back my keys. "I was second string in the NFL. I didn't make millions like some of the others."

"Uh huh."

"Mister Carlisle pays well."

"Uh huh."

"What's wrong?"

I started and tore my eyes away from the man I really needed to get to know better. "Sorry."

"Anyway, I'll see ya, okay? Knock 'em dead!" Bert gave me a pat on the shoulder before leaving.

I glanced around the empty flat. That was nuts.

Without waiting any longer, I hurried into the shower. A quick scrub later and I was in front of my closet. The doorbell chimed.

"Who..." I stayed still, listening. It chimed again. "...is that?"

Worried that it might be Blaire, I hurried to the front of the flat and edged closer to the window. I peeked out and saw an unknown car in the driveway, blocking the garage, and a brunette with a rolling suitcase waited at the door. It wasn't Blaire.

In confusion, I went to the speaker system as the door chimed again. I pushed the button to talk. "Who is it?"

"Olivia? It's Pat. I'm here to do your hair and makeup."

Pat! She had been the mastermind behind my appearance when I went to the first business meeting with Hunter.

I eagerly pushed the button to buzz her in and opened the door. I heard her clomping up the steps. She was looking around with appreciative eyes when she reached the landing. "Nice place. You've moved up in the world."

"It's Hunter's. This is his solution to not wanting to spend the night in my old place."

"Don't blame him. That apartment was a *disaster*." She wheeled her suitcase into the living room and whistled. "This is definitely Hunter. Look at all this space. You're a lucky girl."

"So he doesn't trust me to do myself up for his mom, huh?" I asked with a grin.

She brought over a chair from the dining room and placed it in the living room area. She lowered her suitcase so it was lying flat before unzipping it and removing makeup items. "He just said you needed help preparing for a special occasion." Preparing, in Pat language, was relaxing. "Get the champagne flowing, girlie, and grab your dress. I want to see what I'm working with."

"I don't think we…" I opened the fridge as the front gate clanged. The door opened a moment later, admitting a red-faced and bustling Janelle.

She looked around, smiled at Pat, and then hurried into the kitchen. "I'm so sorry I'm late," she called. "The bus just stopped for no reason and told us all to get out—I had to walk eight blocks!"

"I didn't even know you were supposed to be here." I wandered to where I could see her. Her upper half was behind the door of the fridge.

"You have my schedule." Janelle took out a bottle of champagne and some chocolate-covered strawberries.

"Have it, yeah. Look at it, no."

"C'mon, let's go," Pat said, shooing me toward my room. "I want to see what you're wearing."

I led her to the back of the flat and left her standing at my bedroom door as I pulled out a sophisticated dress in deep, sparkly blue. I laid it on the bed as I pulled out some jewelry to go with it.

"Shoes?" Pat asked, analyzing the selection.

I pulled out some black heels, and then a pair of strappy sandals. "One of these."

"Black heels. It will age you just a little. You don't want to seem too young and hip with a parent. Okay. I think I got it."

"Did Hunter have any directions?" The last time Pat had helped me, Hunter had a very precise way he wanted me to look. Turned out his ideas were perfect and looked awesome. He knew how to look the part better than anyone I knew.

"Nope. He's pretty laid-back about this one. It surprised me." She glanced at my robe. "Put on something not so fluffy and meet me in the living room. Let's get started."

It took Pat an hour and a half to get me looking like a million dollars. The woman was a genius of the highest degree. Hunter arrived halfway through the transformation, grabbed a glass of brandy, asked Janelle to make him something to eat, and escaped to the bedroom.

"And the finishing touches…" Pat fastened the jewelry on and dropped the shoes at my feet. When everything was ready, she and Janelle stepped back.

"Lovely!" Janelle exclaimed, smiling.

Pat smiled, too. "Perfect. You'll knock 'em dead."

"I'll get Mr. Carlisle," Janelle said, walking toward the back of the flat.

Butterflies filled my stomach at what came next. "Oh God, I'm going to meet his mother."

"Relax. You're smart and sweet—you'll do fine." Pat sat on the couch with a glass of champagne.

Hunter came into the room wearing a casual dress shirt without a tie. The deep cream hugged his cut chest and cinched down his trim waist perfectly before tucking into black slacks. I closed my eyes as his delicious smell hit me, his cologne mixing with his natural scent, distinctly man. Safe, protective, and mine.

I smiled as he stopped in front of me. His gaze took in my dress, my accessories, and finally stopped on my eyes. "Perfect. You look beautiful."

"Thanks," I said, reaching forward and slipping my hand in his.

He held it for a moment, squeezing before checking the time. "Shall we?"

The butterflies came back in force. I blew out a breath and gulped down the last of my champagne. "Okay."

"Here." Pat hopped up and handed me a nude shade of lipstick. "Remember to reapply."

"Got it." I took my clutch from Janelle before turning so she could drape a wrap over me. Hunter shrugged into a leather jacket and waited for me by the door.

"You ladies going to just hang out?" I asked as I made my way to Hunter.

"Yeah. There's all these appetizers Janelle made, not to mention champagne—" Pat resettled on the couch.

I looked at Hunter. We always had Janelle and Mrs. Foster in the flat, but it was weird for Pat to assume she could hang when the owners were gone.

Hunter answered my reservations by winking and slipping his hand around my waist. "Ready?" he asked quietly.

I shrugged. "Sure." I waved at the ladies and let him guide me down to the garage and into his car.

"You're driving this time, huh?" I asked as the garage door opened and he started the car.

"Yes. There is plenty of parking."

"And you don't mind Pat staying in the house when we're not there?"

"No. I've known her for a long time. I trust her, and I trust Janelle. They'll look after things. It's no different

139

than leaving Kimberly behind."

That made sense.

He paused in the driveway as the garage door closed. I could see his lips thin as his eyes trained on the pink scrawl. He didn't say anything, though, just waited until the garage was fully closed before backing out.

Hunter's mother lived across the Golden Gate Bridge in a stupidly wealthy area where a large house would be priced in the millions. Not a mansion, just a large house. It was the area where all the wealthy people, who worked in downtown San Francisco in extremely well-paying jobs, lived.

"I just can't get behind the idea of an area where you spend millions on a normal-sized house. You could have a palace in middle America for this kind of money."

"But then you'd have to live in middle America." Hunter parked the car in between a shiny Mercedes and a Tesla, and across the street from a Porsche.

"What's wrong with middle America?" I didn't make a move to get out of the car. Even if I looked like one of them, they'd be able to sniff me out, easily. I was from modest stock, and rich people could tell.

"Snow, sleet, cold, not to mention landlocked—need I continue?" Hunter smiled at me and got out of the car.

I was pretty sure a little snow would be a small price to pay for affordable housing, but I couldn't tell that to someone who owned an island. He just wouldn't get it.

The door opened, allowing a swirl of cold air into the car. I pulled my wrap tighter around me before I took

Hunter's hand to get out of his sleek sports car. "I forgot that the temperature shifts by ten degrees across the bridge."

"At least. It's chilly here."

I smoothed my dress and then looked around again. "I feel like Cinderella. I'll probably have to pull a runner in a few hours when everyone realizes I still have something called college debt…"

"Not Cinderella." Hunter put his arm around my shoulders as we walked up the walkway to the front door. "Belle from *Beauty and the Beast*. You were smart and beautiful before I found you. The only change you made was putting on nice clothes and jewelry. It's still the same you. I was the one who turned from something ugly into something I hope, one day, you'll be proud of. The transformation was all on my side. Because of you."

I leaned into him as warmth filled my chest. He squeezed me tight as we arrived at the door. He turned me to him, lifting my chin so he could give me a soft kiss. He looked into my eyes for a moment before giving me a smile, then rang the doorbell.

"You don't just walk in?" I asked, savoring the soft look he'd just given me. Trying to commit to memory the beautiful words.

"Do you just walk into your mother's house?"

"No, but your mother likes you. Right?"

He squeezed me close again. "She likes to hang on to ceremony with these types of things. Besides, her butler insists on the *right* way to do things."

"She has a butler?" I mumbled as the door swung open slowly.

An old man that may or may not have already died and refused to admit it stood in the doorway wearing a black suit and a bright red bowtie. Wrinkles lined his face and white wisps of hair stuck out from his head. "Mr. Carlisle. How nice to see you. And Miss Jonston, I presume?"

"Mr. Smith, hello. How are you?" Hunter guided me forward as the butler stepped back to admit us before closing the door behind us.

"Just fine, Mr. Carlisle. Just fine. May I take your wrap, miss?"

Hunter shrugged out of his jacket as the oldest butler in the world draped my wrap across a coat hanger, moving so slowly a turtle would be impatient.

"Please, follow me." Mr. Smith led us down a wide hall adorned with well-polished furniture and really neat art. My gaze was captured by a painting and became trapped, following the colors and lines within the frame.

Despite the fact that everything seemed high-dollar and of the best quality, it gave the impression of having been bought long ago and kept in good condition. The style, and an occasional faded color or two, lent it that older person feel that said Hunter's mom hadn't updated her furnishings in a while. Not that she really needed to—it all still looked great. Just...dated.

When did I start noticing this type of stuff?

"You were raised here?" I asked quietly as we made

our way through a large room and toward the low murmur of voices.

"Partly. My mother had a large estate in Arizona."

"Had?"

"She had to sell in the divorce."

"Why Arizona? Talk about landlocked…"

"That's where she grew up."

We entered a large room where a crystal chandelier hung from the middle of the ceiling. About twelve people were gathered, all in shirts or dresses. Everyone but us were in their later years, something I could tell by the loose folds in their necks or the liver spots on their hands. Faces were a different story, though. Most of the women looked ten years younger, at least, than their bodies. The men were the same, genteel and sophisticated.

"Who has the fountain of youth in their backyard?" I asked Hunter as the butler bowed and slowly left the room. He was like wrinkles on a couple sticks badly held together.

A middle-aged woman in a caterer's suit with a black bowtie and a blank expression approached. "Can I get you two something to drink?" she asked.

Hunter looked at me, indicating I should answer first. "Champagne, please."

"Scotch for me. Neat." Hunter waited for the woman to nod and disappear before he said, "My mother has youthful friends. As you can see, they keep themselves in shape."

Now that he mentioned it, I saw that he was right. Women and men alike were slim or average, none overweight, and only one on the stockier side. They didn't loaf around, either, unlike the butler. They moved well and easily, laughing often and smiling most of the time.

I straightened up a little. They also all had great posture.

"Hunter, dear." A striking lady approached us with a slight smile. Her elegantly spiky hair said "fashionable" and her glimmering black dress screamed "sophisticated." She had the same trim physique and ageless appearance as the others, highlighting this with mostly nude makeup. Her jewelry was similar in style, size, and cut to mine.

And now I knew where Hunter got his style and taste. He'd learned from a master. Thank God he'd arranged for Pat to come over!

"Mother." Hunter gave his mom a light kiss to her cheek. He stepped back and turned to me, slipping his arm around my shoulders. "This is Olivia. Livy, this is my mother, Trisha."

"Hello." Trisha put out a hand as her hazel eyes sparkled. "It is so nice to finally meet someone that has Hunter's affection. He doesn't usually bring anyone around."

Except Blaire, as she had been invited...

"Hi." I shook her hand, trying to match her light, soft tone and the grip. I figured mimicking her in manners would be my best bet. "It's nice to meet you. I've heard a lot about you."

"Oh. That's nice." Trisha looked at her son fondly, patting him on the shoulder. She turned back to me. "Where are my manners? I'll take you for a tour while Hunter gets his business out of the way early."

"You know me too well, Mother." To me he said, "I just want to talk to one of my mother's advisors about an investment. Will you be okay for a few minutes?"

"Sure. Of course." Nervous jitters made my hands shake, forcing me to clasp them in front of me so as not to betray my lie. I didn't want to be left alone with his mom—she'd figure out I was a fraud and probably tell her son to run away screaming.

"Great." Surprising me, Hunter gave me a light kiss to the temple before he took his arm away.

Chapter 12

"LOVELY." TRISHA WAITED for Hunter to move away before politely putting out her hand, gesturing me toward the right. "And where did you grow up?"

I nearly had to lean in to hear her. "Just north of here—San Rafael."

"Oh yes, of course. Beautiful area, like this one. A bit more removed from the fog and chill of the city."

"Yes. Summers get warm there, unlike San Francisco."

We walked down a hall, slowing in front of a painting. Trisha stopped with a patient smile, letting me take a look before walking slowly on.

"Did you decorate?" I asked, uncomfortable with the silence.

"In part. When I first moved, I used an interior designer, but I gave my input."

"Hmm. Mhm." I clasped my hands behind my back, searching for something else to talk about. Despite what I'd said, Hunter really hadn't said much about his mother. I had no idea what she did for fun, if she liked jokes, what she did with her day—I had no basis for a conversation, and asking basic questions might prove my earlier lie.

"Do you go into the city often?" I said as we paused near another piece of art, this one a painting of a statue beside an explosion of flowers.

"Not often, no. I shop there on occasion, but it is awfully busy."

"Yes. Very congested. I used to live downtown, which was great, as I don't have a car. I could walk everywhere I needed to go—everything was right there. I was used to all the people. But now I live out near the ocean, and while it's still kind of busy, it's way slower out there. Downtown seems much busier to me now."

We climbed the stairs and turned left at the top. I had never been on a tour of anything with so few words. In all reality, I could've seen and learned a whole lot more if I'd just wandered around on my own. She wasn't describing the pictures or telling me any family history. Heck, she wasn't even grilling me about her son. Even though she seemed really laid-back and extremely genteel, I was starting to get more than a little uncomfortable.

"This is my favorite piece," Trisha said quietly as she clicked on the hall light.

I dutifully looked at the mess of a painting on the wall. Then leaned a little closer, not believing this had actually been put on sale.

A creature of some sort sat on a blob of brown. A man on a log? He held a gray sluglike thing. In front of him was a large, round blue area. Within it were strange shapes of all colors, one looking close to a five-year-old's attempt at a fish. At the top was a round sun with the customary lines for rays.

The thing looked like a child painted it, for cripes' sakes. And it probably cost millions.

"Oh. Wow." I nodded and smiled. "It's really interesting."

Trisha gave me that soft smile. "Yes. A lovely attempt by Hunter when he was six. He wanted to be a painter at the time."

My mouth dropped. My smile turned into a wry grin. "Get out!" I stepped closer, seeing that the brown smudge was a dock, not a log, and he was, indeed, trying to draw fish. "Wow. I had no idea he had been a budding artist."

"Oh no, he was never any good." Trisha moved down the hallway to another mess of a painting, this one depicting a camping scene with a big brown blob in the far right. The dotted white of stars stretched across a streaked black sky. A burning flame, fairly well done, twisted up from strange greenish...sticks? Another creature, definitely supposed to be a human, sat with a tree trunk next to him. A squiggly gray line was on the other side.

"Fishing pole," I said, pointing to the tree-trunk-looking thing. "Fish." I pointed to the gray line. "Fire, stars—I have all that. What's the brown blob?"

"A bear, I believe."

"Oohhhh." I nodded, chuckling. "A nature scene with an element of danger."

I heard Trisha's soft laugh as she led the way to the young Hunter's next masterpiece. This one was a meadow under an orange sky streaked with pink. A half circle of yellow with hazy rays lay on the picture's horizon. The green foreground had various colored dots, some representational of flowers, and some a lazy attempt to fill up the page.

"Looks like he got tired of making flowers..." I pointed out the examples.

"Yes. He didn't have the constitution of a painter."

My eyes slid over the painting. "This one is way better than the others. It actually portrays a feeling. There's kind of a...sweetness to it."

"He was a few years older when he did this one. It was his last. His dad pushed him toward money and business shortly after he finished this piece."

"Well, I'm sure he's way better at business than he was at painting, but...it's kind of a shame he let go of the hobby. He doesn't have any hobbies now. Or none that I know of. Even golf is for business."

"Exactly. And if you'll notice, all these are outdoor pictures. Wild, wilderness. He did so love to play in the dirt. He was always begging me to go camping. He has a fondness for the outdoors that, sadly, I never indulged. I regret that now."

I glanced back at the other pictures before looking again at the meadow. It was true—fishing, sitting beside a roaring fire under the stars, and finally, when he was older, a beautiful meadow filled with wildflowers at sunset. He had none of that now. No nature. Hardly even a yard, actually.

Trisha continued down the hall. I followed, my mind whirling.

"I used to like camping," I said, remembering my own childhood. "My dad took me a lot. I was really good at fishing—very patient. I didn't touch the fish once I caught them, though. My dad dealt with the hook and cleaning it and all that. It was fun. Those were good times."

"Maybe you can take Hunter one day—show him what he's missing." Trisha clicked another switch and light showered a guy's room. There was a picture of a sports car on the wall with a half-naked woman leaning against it, sticking out her huge boobs. A desk off to the right had an old computer, some pens and paper, and a stack of magazines. I bet that if I lifted the mattress, I'd find a nude magazine.

"Hunter's room?" I asked in disbelief.

"Yes. I kept it as he left it. Not quite what you would expect…"

"Uh, *no*! I can't believe he left that picture of the car up. He would've been old enough to know how clichéd that was…"

"Men don't notice things when they've no need to. If

he didn't have assistants now, you would know he was a bachelor. For all his attempts to be a grown man, he has the traits of a teenage boy. I'm convinced they all do until they have a wife who makes them grow up."

"Hunter seems plenty grown up." I shook my head, unable to help myself, and lifted the mattress.

"I had that removed. But you are correct—boys aren't always as sneaky as they think they are."

"Not as sneaky as women, anyway." I laughed, walking back toward Trisha. "My mind is blown."

"Hunter was forced to grow up. His trouble with his father made sure of that. I have every belief, however, that having a baby, and raising a child, will remind him of some very good years. It would be good for him."

I couldn't believe what I was hearing. It sounded suspiciously like she meant me. Like he would have a child with *me*. I'd just met this woman and Hunter wouldn't even say he loved me—what was she smoking that she thought this was a good idea? I could just have been after what was in his bank account for all she knew.

She met my gaze and smiled. "He is too serious these days, don't you agree?" She turned, not waiting for an answer, and led the way back out of the room.

I followed with numb limbs. This situation had just become completely surreal. "I think he is afraid of having kids," I mumbled.

"He is afraid to make the mistakes his parents made. He needs an intelligent woman who cares for him deeply to reassure him. I worried he would never find one, with his lack of social life. I'm delighted he is looking at other options."

Often people were worried about getting the approval of their boyfriend's parents. Not me. I was worried about one trying to hit on me, and the other using me as a baby factory. One wanted to strip his son of everything his son loved, and the other wanted to shove love in his face.

Hunter was right—there was no normalcy here. His parents were nuts.

My mom might not have cared about me until Hunter walked in, but then I was suddenly invited to her party. *All* her parties.

All of our parents were nuts.

Hunter looked up as we returned to the gathering, his eyes tight and his face devoid of expression. I had one moment of confusion before I heard the laugh and recognized the gorgeous woman standing beside him.

Blaire said something to a tall man she was talking to before draping her hand on Hunter's arm. Her dress fit her snugly, showing off her stellar body. The top swooped low, giving her ample chest plenty of breathing room, and a slit showed all the way to her mid-thigh. The woman was a knockout, but a little too scantily dressed for this crowd, thank God.

"I do so apologize for inviting his former...ward," Trisha said in a low tone laced with distaste. "I had not spoken to him before I sent out the invitation."

"She's...no fun," I replied.

Hunter stepped toward me as I closed the distance, his mom by my side. Blaire's hand dropped when Hunter moved away, and she looked over.

Fiery hate crouched in her glittering eyes as she saw me. She gave my dress the briefest of glances and smirked.

"Trisha! Hi!" Blaire gave Trisha a giant smile. She kissed the older woman on the cheek. "You are looking *great!*"

"Thank you, Blaire. It's lovely to see you again."

"Yes. And thank you for the invitation. It's been so long."

Hunter stepped up beside me and threaded his hand around my waist. He pulled me in close.

"I was just telling Hunter the other day—"

Blaire cut off for a second as Hunter moved us away. She started talking again a moment later, but I lost track of what she was saying.

"Did you see my failed career as an artist?" Hunter asked, moving through the room, away from everyone else.

"You knew she'd show me that, huh?"

He stopped next to a large window. Cool, smooth blackness pressed against the other side. He turned to me, his eyes delving into mine. "Yes. She's been dying to show someone those. All her new friends see those first."

"She thinks I should take you camping." I ran my hand up his hard chest, wanting to tell him she also thought he should start a family, and that I wanted him to start it with me.

"We'd get eaten by bears." His eyes glittered down as his lips tweaked up at the corners.

I fell into his gaze, lost in those velvety brown eyes. "Or so your painting would have me believe."

"I was telling the future. That's why I never went camping—I knew what would happen."

I smiled, stepping closer. Heat warmed between our bodies. I angled my face up as he looked down on me. His eyes trained on my lips. "Livy..." he said quietly, his breath brushing my face. His hands clutched my back, shaking a little. A small amount of fear wormed into his gaze, but it was drowned out by something else. Something I also felt, and longed to say. "I luu—"

"Hunter, you bad boy!"

Hunter jerked with Blaire's voice, his head snapping up.

She sauntered slowly toward us, her hips moving more than should be possible while still walking in a straight line. "It's time for dinner. Didn't you hear the bell?"

Hunter dropped his hands, still standing close to me. "I didn't."

Blaire stopped and turned, waiting for us to follow along. Her thin eyebrows lifted. "Well? Let's go, silly! We don't want to keep everyone waiting. It's rude..."

"Of course." Hunter's tone had dropped, coarse and expressionless. It was the voice he hid his emotions behind, showing the world a robot.

His hand settled on the small of my back as he guided me forward, passing Blaire.

"What? You're not going to escort a lady into dinner?" she asked in a light tone hiding razor blades.

Hunter's body went rigid for a moment before he stopped. He put out his hand like a man might have done in an old western, waiting for her to take it. He moved his hand from my back and held out his arm the same way for me.

"This still happens, huh? This leading women to dinner thing?" I mumbled, taking his arm.

"Oh, Hunter, didn't you school her about polite society before you brought her here with your mother's closest friends?" Blaire laughed in a condescending way. "You have your work cut out for you there."

Little did she know, I'd seen *Titanic* twice. I knew the drill.

We walked through the room and into the large dining room with crystal and china set out along the table. Two vacant seats were on the other side of the table, each with a little white card in front of it. A single space stood in front of us, the little white card reading "Blaire" in beautiful script.

I heard Blaire *tsk* as Hunter left her in front of her place and continued around the table to the two open seats.

"Sorry about that," Hunter said as he pulled out the chair for me.

"Not at all. If it's good enough for the *Titanic*, it's

good enough for me."

He gave me a quizzical look.

"They did that in the movie—leading ladies to dinner... Never mind." I put my napkin in my lap as he sat beside me.

As everyone settled down, servers poured wine and water. Trisha said, "Welcome, everyone, and thank you so much for coming!"

Smiles and returned thanks murmured around the table. She continued, "As I'm sure you know, we have a new addition to our party. Please welcome Olivia. She has taken on the nearly impossible task of keeping my son in line."

Everyone laughed. The woman next to Hunter patted his forearm.

"Lovely to meet you," the man next to me said. He stuck out his large, callused hand. I'd noticed him earlier, as the stockiest person of the group, but it was now clear that his larger frame came from muscle rather than being padded with fat. "I'm Mike."

I shook his hand, noticing how rough it was, as though he'd worked outside all his life. "Hi."

"And what do you do?" Mike asked with a pleasant smile.

"Oh, I work—"

"Yes, Olivia." The clear voice rang out for the whole table to hear. Blaire looked at me with malicious, sparkling eyes. "What *do* you do?" Blaire turned to the man next to her. "I've met Olivia before, but never had a chance to talk to her properly."

The man smiled politely and looked at me, giving me his undivided attention. In fact, the whole table had, apparently eager to get to know the new person. Swell.

I swallowed nervously. Hunter's hand came to rest on my thigh. "I work for Hunter, actually. That's how I met him."

"And what is it you do for Hunter?" Blaire asked with a light but knowing tone.

"I'm his assistant," I said, feeling my stack of debt. These people *had* assistants; they *weren't* assistants. I didn't fit in, and I'd just admitted it.

"Livy majored in Computer Engineering at Stanford and fell victim to the economy," Hunter added in a nonchalant voice. Many of those at the table groaned and shifted, nodding in understanding. "She tried to refuse my job offer, but as you know, I'm a man who gets what he wants…"

Mike laughed in a booming voice as a server slid a salad in front of him. "Still haven't got hold of my company, young man! I'm holding out."

"Not yet, no," Hunter said, leaning back so a server could place a salad in front of him. "But you'll retire soon enough. I don't have long to wait."

"Mike will never retire. He has his life in that company!" a man down the table added with a smile. "It's like a kid, but it never rebels."

"Oh, it tried to rebel. The economy hit us pretty hard, too. We had to make some big cuts—running lean now. Not a lot of work coming through." Mike picked up his fork as he looked at me. "I own a construction business. I built it from the ground up. Started out with nothing but blood, sweat, and tears, and now I get jobs from all across the nation. You have to start somewhere."

"Hear, hear." The man down the table raised his glass.

"Olivia doesn't do traditional assistant work for me," Hunter said as he put his glass down and picked up his fork, eyeing his salad. "She's no good at it."

My mouth dropped open in disbelief as Trisha said, "Hunter! That is no way to talk about—"

"I'm not saying that as a fault," Hunter hastened to say, raising his hands to stop his mother's rebuff. "But when you show her a spreadsheet, she forgets about lunch plans, meetings, plane tickets—all her focus is taken by that spreadsheet. Organizing schedules is not her strong suit, which works out well for me. I have a fantastic EA for those needs. With Olivia, I hand her tasks that might take a week if I passed them to the correct department. With her, I get them in a day. I'm spoiled."

"Code, not spreadsheets," I muttered. Nobody noticed.

"I was never any good at organizing, either," Mike said in a kind voice, and winked at me.

"She is working on a project with the owner of a company we are taking over," Hunter continued in a strong voice. "They're developing a game app."

"A game app?" Trisha inquired.

"It's a video game that's meant to be played on your smart phone," I clarified, picking at my salad. "The app will be free to download, but after a certain number of levels you'll have to pay to continue."

"That's where they get ya!" a woman with bright red lipstick said at the end of the table opposite Trisha. "I play a couple of puzzle games my daughter downloaded to my phone. They're very addictive."

"What kind of game are you designing?" a woman with nearly white hair next to Hunter asked.

"I've convinced him to make it a type of puzzle game with a war theme. Violent games do extremely well right now, so we're going to start with that. If it does well, we'll come out with another game that is more puzzle than war for those who like nonviolent games."

"Oh, I don't like those shoot-'em-up games all the kids are playing." The woman with red lipstick shook her head adamantly and reached for her wine.

"When will you release?" Mike asked as Trisha and another couple people murmured about the shoot-'em-up games.

"In about a month, I think. We're nearly ready." I smiled with the excitement I always felt when talking about the game. "We've worked really hard on it. You never know how it'll do, of course. It could flop and then all that time would be wasted. But hopefully it won't."

"It won't flop," the woman next to Hunter said with a reassuring smile.

"Looks like you love that line of work." Mike eyed me with a steady gaze. "Even if it doesn't work for you, it's a good hobby. You should always strive to do what you love."

"Since when do you love pushing a shovel around?" a graying man with a smile said.

"I get a young buck to work the shovel. But there's nothing like working in the outdoors. Or standing at the foot of a building that you helped build." Mike put his fork on his half-empty plate and pushed it forward. A server came to clear it immediately. "I've always loved to build. To make things with my hands. What a wonderful thing to get to do what you love. Young Hunter here hasn't realized that yet. But he will. Then he'll *really* perform miracles."

"You're incorrect. I do love what I do. I've always loved business," Hunter said.

"You love business, but you don't love reporting to a committee of pompous, snooty types, isn't that right?" Mike leaned forward so he could see Hunter around me.

Hunter chewed, looking straight ahead. He didn't respond.

As if Hunter's silence was answer enough, Mike nodded. To me, he said, "Hunter loves to build, too. He loves to take a company that's faltering and make it into something slick and shiny. You know how I know this?"

Mike looked around the table. All eyes were on him. "He came to buy out my company when it was in the worst shape. Mismanaged, tons of problems—hell, I didn't know what I was doing. I'll admit it. He saw the potential, saw what it would take to get it on the right track, and wanted to push up his sleeves and get to work. His sales pitch?" Mike's gaze went around me to Hunter again. "'Let me build your company the right way so you can build your dream.' Well, he was talking about high rises. That was always my dream—build a grand high rise in a bustling city."

Mike leaned back and wiped his mouth. He gave a smile as he continued. "I wouldn't sell. I was just about bankrupt, but it was *my* company. I wanted to see it through, right or wrong—I was a bit stubborn back then..." More than a few people snorted at that. "That was when I realized Hunter was more like his mother than his father. He helped me anyway. As a family friend, he rolled up his sleeves. He got into the trenches with me without ever asking what he would get in return. He gave me advice a young man shouldn't know, not even with another twenty years' experience. He showed me the right path, and he helped me stay on it. Still does, as a matter of fact. He owns a quarter of the company now, but if I'm honest, he should get credit for half."

"My advice wasn't insightful, it was logic. You were just too busy with your hammers and nails to realize it," Hunter said in a soft voice, laying down his fork on an almost empty plate.

Mike scoffed. "Yeah, right. You don't have to pretend to be humble in front of your girlfriend..."

Hunter's lips threatened a shy smile. He slipped his hand back onto my thigh.

Mike watched the server deliver the next course before he said, "When he finally does get to build his dream company, watch out, world. That thing will take off."

"So when Olivia's hard work takes off, Hunter can step in and build her an empire." The woman with red lipstick smiled. "I miss the days of young love, when you had your whole lives ahead of you."

"What are you talking about—you still look sixteen!" the graying man said in a booming voice.

"Oh!" The woman with the red lipstick touched her hair with a delighted smile. "Don't I wish."

"I don't. I was poor and clueless." Mike laughed.

Everyone laughed as the conversations broke up, people turning to talk to those closest. As I took a bite of my lamb, I noticed Blaire's eyes on me, burning with hatred. Her plans to ostracize me from the group had failed.

For a woman that liked to win, she didn't do it very often…

I'd probably see her wrath eventually, but right now, I just wanted to enjoy Hunter's family and friends. He was opening up another little part of himself, and I was eager to become a part of it.

Chapter 13

THE REST OF the dinner party went surprisingly well. Trisha's friends were cordial and polite, easy to talk to and always friendly. They were never once snobby, and no one seemed to care about my background. Aside from Blaire constantly trying to be wherever Hunter was, and always trying to butt into his conversations, I had a great time.

The next week went quickly, with a haze of work blending the days together. It turned out Bruce and I were a lot closer to launching the app than I'd originally thought. We had a few tweaks and some coding problems, but a beta test had actually gone out to a select group of computer geeks. They'd be harder on our game than normal people, but they'd also find ninety-nine percent of the bugs.

This meant, of course, that Bruce was more hyped up and anxious than normal, sending me fixes and issues throughout the day. I took lunch breaks just to work on his notes. The moment I left Hunter, I was working for

Bruce. It was brutal.

When the next Saturday rolled around, I was in my home office with the stack of boxes, staring at the computer with puffy eyes. I entered the last few lines of code, tried to think of anything else I could possibly have to do, and then fell back in my chair with a huge sigh.

"*Finally!*" I rubbed my tired eyes. That should keep Bruce off my back for a few days. Maybe.

I checked the time. Hunter would probably be over soon. Hopefully.

I thought back to his almost-admission from the week before. He had been going to say he loved me. It had to be. He hadn't said anything since, but I often saw that emotion in his eyes. The emotion he'd had when he started to say the word. It was just a matter of time.

I turned around and stared at the stack of boxes. What a pain. I hated unpacking. I wouldn't even need most of the stuff. Janelle had stocked the flat pretty well.

My gaze roamed over the various boxes, as I tried to figure out where to start, when it snagged on two boxes at the bottom. A chill passed up my spine as I stared at the word "bathroom" printed on the side.

"Oh shit," I whispered, getting up with wooden movements.

My phone rang. I barely heard it.

Like a zombie, I moved one box after the other, working down to that "bathroom" box. Once there, I ripped it open and rifled through it.

It didn't have what I was looking for.

I found the next and did the same, pushing past some bath towels to find my little blue canvas bag. I took it out and stared at it.

I had been a week without taking the pill. And not the sugar pill week, either, where your body and Aunt Flow battle, cramps make your life miserable, and you just wait for the end. No. The week *after* that.

I'd had sex nearly every day. Unprotected.

What the fuck had I been *thinking?*

I *never* forgot the pill. Never! I was religious about it. Always had been. I'd never even had a scare before, I was that conscientious.

Yet this last week it hadn't crossed my mind once. Not once.

I groaned.

Hunter had trusted me. This was such a big deal, and Hunter had trusted me with it in a way he hadn't trusted anyone else. But aside from that, *what the fuck was I thinking?*

Hyperventilating, I walked out to the living room. Once there, I wiped my suddenly damp forehead and sat on the couch. My phone rang in my office again.

I had to tell him. There was no way around that. We'd have to use condoms for the rest of the month, and he'd want to know why.

My stomach churned. The good news was that I probably wasn't pregnant yet. Ovulation happened more toward the middle of the cycle. *I think.*

I got up and paced in the middle of the living room.

He was supposed to be home in an hour or so and we were going shopping for God-knew-what. Naturally, I should just wait until he got home, admit my mistake, and assure him we were probably fine.

Fear worked through my body and out through my limbs. I shook out my hands. He had every right to be extremely pissed off about this. I had majorly screwed up. This wasn't one of those situations where both parties were equally to blame; this was all down to me. I'd assumed responsibility, assured him I was trustworthy, and then been negligent.

I started back to my office, thinking that working might distract me until Hunter got home. I could do some things for Hunter. Or go over that code again for Bruce. I didn't have high hopes that it would work, but pacing in the middle of the floor wasn't doing any good.

As I passed the door, I heard the gate of the building clang. I froze. It could be anyone. Janelle often stopped by on her day off—maybe she'd forgotten something. Or maybe Mrs. Foster had…

I watched the door handle turn before the door swung open. In stepped an incredibly handsome man with a tailored suit, loosened tie, and sexy bedroom eyes.

"Why are you home so early?" I said in a hoarse voice.

A crease formed between Hunter's eyebrows. His expression turned into one of confusion as he closed the door behind him. "Are you okay?"

"You're home early," I said again.

"What's the matter?" Hunter walked toward me, reaching out to brush his hands across my cheek when he neared.

I flinched, fear clawing at me. Tears came to my eyes. "I fucked up, Hunter. I fucked up really bad."

"Hey." He grabbed me, pulling me into his body. "What happened?"

I pushed against him, struggling out of his grip. A terrified, angry tear rolled down my cheek. I wiped it away as my chin trembled. "I forgot to take the pill. All week I forgot. I've been without protection."

Fear welled up again, not just from what he might say or do, but from the uncertainty of what that just might mean. I was young, just starting out, and had no solid ties to the man in front of me. If he fired me, I would immediately go back to unemployed with a mountain of debt. How could I possibly raise a child, too? How could I afford it, much less grow up to nurture it? I could barely take care of myself!

"It might be okay," I said, mostly to myself. I wiped my tears with a trembling hand. "I don't think I ovulate until the middle of the month. So if we use condoms now, I think we'll be okay. We should. I'm pretty sure. I'm really sorry—there's no excuse. I just...I have no idea how I forgot. I really don't. I was looking for them two weeks ago, and meant to come back, and then it was my period week, so that was fine, and then, somehow..."

A hiccup interrupted my babbling. I sniffled and wiped my hand across my face. "I just remembered today. I was thinking about all the boxes behind me and then…"

I looked up through my lashes. Hunter stood motionless, staring at me with a straight face and rigid body. This was the expression and stance he used to distance himself from what was going on around him. Still he didn't speak.

I let my shoulders slump as I swallowed back a sob. "You trusted me. I know that. I broke that trust. But please believe me, Hunter, I didn't mean to. I really didn't. I honestly don't know how I could forget. I *never* forget about that kind of stuff. Not even when I'm not sexually active—I've never forgotten before."

A sob racked my body as I withered within his stare. I threw up my hands helplessly. "I don't know what I can do right now. What's done is done. And I accept it if you—"

"Is it mine—would it be mine?"

"Wh-what?" I managed.

"If you did get pregnant. Would it be mine?"

My face dropped. I was incredulous. "What do you mean, would it be *yours*? Who else's would it be?"

"That's what I'm asking."

"Of *course* it would be yours. I don't think God plants babies in women like me."

In a flash of memory, I realized why he was asking. The last time he thought he might be a father, it had actually been his dad's baby. He'd been lied to, and it had killed him.

"Sorry—when you ask a question like that, it sounds like you're accusing me of cheating. I mean…you are, but…I get why." I wiped away another tear. "Yes, you're the only man I've been with since the beginning. And before that I was on a dry spell, so if the worst happens, it'll have your DNA."

"I have your word? I trust you, Olivia, but I need to hear you say it."

I huffed, fresh tears springing to my eyes. "You did trust me, yes. And look where it got you. But yeah, it'd be yours."

I heard Hunter exhale before he gathered me up into his strong arms. "Okay."

"What do you mean, 'okay'?" I mumbled, curling up in his arms. I needed love right now. I needed support and encouragement, because I was terrified what might happen. What it would mean in my life.

"I mean that this is okay." He pulled his upper body back and ran his fingers along my jaw line, applying pressure to make me look up. His eyes were soft and deep. "I love you. I didn't think I'd ever love again, but since I first saw you, you pulled at me. You sucked me in. I can't live without you, Olivia Jonston. I've found in you what I've always wanted in a woman. You turned me from a heartless bastard, living in a colorless world, into someone who sees the beauty in everyday life. You've taught me to feel again. I've never been this happy, in my life."

More tears rolled down my cheeks, and not from fear

this time.

He smiled and leaned down, kissing the trails of moisture. "My mother loves you, too. It took her the same amount of time to see in you what I do. She knew you had a hold on me from the first, and she knows I'll never let you go."

"I thought you were just waiting for me to realize you were awful and take off?" I huffed out a laugh.

He laid his hand against my cheek. "I'm afraid I'd follow you. I can't let you go—it isn't in me. You have me wrapped around your finger, and I'd bend whichever way I needed to make you happy." He wiped my cheek with his thumb.

I took a deep, shuddering breath. "But what about the lack of protection issue?"

"I'm ready. I've always wanted kids—why not start now?"

I shook my head a fraction, the fear from a few moments before still coursing through me, but now love and joy were fighting it. "You're supposed to be angry."

He smiled and pulled me into his chest. "I'm not. Not at all. You've been stressed, busy—plus, you did ask me to help you get the box out. I knew what you were looking for, and I forgot all about it. So you see, it's not just your fault."

I tucked my face into his chest. "I'm not really ready yet, Hunter."

"We'll use protection from now on, and just see what happens, okay? But let's not worry about what we can't control. There's no point in it."

I closed my eyes and took a big breath, soaking in his heat and assurance that everything would work out. "Okay."

"Now. Let's get changed. I want to go shopping, and then we can go out for a late lunch or early dinner."

I reached up and gently grabbed his face, turning it down to me. He bent, knowing what I wanted, and captured my lips. I opened my mouth, moaning when he filled it with his tongue. One more time wouldn't matter…

Urgency overcame me. I stepped back, pulling him with me. My fingers tore at his shirt, popping a button open and pulling another off. Two more followed, skidding against the floor. I ripped at his pants, yanking them open and shoving them down.

His hands slid under my shirt and pushed my bra up, cupping my breasts. His palms rubbed against my hard nipples and sent shooting sparks of pleasure through my body.

"Take me, Hunter," I begged, undoing my pants and pushing them down. I shimmied out of them, hooking a thigh high on his hip and pulling him closer.

His erection hit off me. He grabbed the base of his cock and directed it to my opening, his lips greedy and insistent on mine. The tip pushed at my wetness. He thrust, sheathing himself to the hilt.

"Hmm," I moaned, clutching at his shoulders.

He grabbed me by my thighs and hoisted me up,

pinning me against the wall. He pulled back and thrust again, starting to build a hard and fast rhythm. I tilted my hips to meet his plunge, and then pulled back, stroking him.

"Yes," he said softly, our breath mingling. Heat blistered between our bodies and unfurled deep inside me.

"I love you, Hunter," I said, my heart thumping with intense emotion, my body reveling in the pleasure of having him inside me.

"I love you," he murmured.

The feelings, both physical and emotional, shocked into me, taking me higher. I held on to his shoulders, moaning into his mouth. Soaking up the exquisite pleasure. Feeling something deep inside that I'd never felt before. Love, pure and sweet, spiraled outward, overcoming me. Flowering between us.

"Hunter," I groaned, kissing him passionately.

His hands tightened on my hips, holding me in place while he plunged into me. I held on with everything I had, my body coiling. The pleasure coalescing. My breath came out in pants. My moans grew louder.

Still the pleasure built.

"Oh," I breathed, rocking against him.

Harder he strove, our bodies crashing together. The sensations tightened in my core. My toes curled.

An orgasm blasted through me. "Oh!" I exalted, shuddering against him.

His body shook against me with his own release. His arms snaked behind me, holding me tight. He buried his head into my neck as he shook again.

I hooked my ankles around his back and draped myself onto him as the last of the pleasure washed through my body.

"Now it's my fault, too." He lightly sucked at the hot skin on my neck. "But really, what's one more day?"

"I think I will blame you for that, just because it makes me feel better. A little."

"Good. Let's shower, and then get going."

"Always in a hurry."

Hunter stepped away from the wall and put me down gently. His expression had turned serious. "We may not have a baby yet, but I'm hoping eventually that we will, Livy. And when that day comes, we can't work this much. Neither of us can. Not if we want to raise a child right. I want to be a good father. I don't want to raise a child like I was raised. So when we do eventually cross that road, God willing, we're going to need to compromise on our work commitment. Promise me that."

"But...you're the one with the high-powered job, Hunter. I work this much because you say I have to."

"You are working two jobs right now."

"Well...yeah. But that's more of a hobby. I don't have to do that."

Doubt flickered across Hunter's features. "Just promise me."

"Sure," I said. "Of course. I'm not going to pass up a man saying he wants to be a good dad."

He kissed me on my forehead and took my hand, ignoring the clothes left on the floor. As we entered the bathroom and Hunter stripped the rest of the way, I couldn't help but wonder. "What are you going to do if you have to scale back working? Something always comes up."

"Change jobs, probably. Maybe start my own company. We'll see."

My eyebrows rose as he turned on the water. "I'm not sure if anyone has mentioned this, but having your own company is often ten times the work."

"That's if they don't know what they're doing."

"Um…" I let the word linger in a way that said, "I don't think that's accurate…"

He obviously caught my drift, because he said, "We'll cross that path when we come to it."

"Bridge." I stripped and followed him into the shower.

"What's that?"

"Bridge. Cross that bridge—never mind."

WITH HUNTER DRIVING, we crossed the Golden Gate Bridge and drove into the heart of Marin. I'd asked Hunter repeatedly what we were shopping for, but he hadn't said. It wasn't until we were pulling into the car lot that I finally figured it out.

"No way. I told you I didn't need a car."

"You're living in a part of the city where a car is essential. You don't have one. Therefore, you need one."

A salesman looked up from a couple he was helping out on the lot. His gaze took in Hunter's expensive ride, and then Hunter himself when he stepped out of the car. I had made him wear jeans, but he wouldn't fool anyone. The Rolex, the Prada sunglasses, the way he wore those jeans—he had money, and this salesman could see it from across the car lot.

Unfortunately for that salesman, though, someone in the building we were parked next to could see it as well. A man in his twenties came out of the glass doors with greased-back hair, a tacky gold watch, and a dress shirt that fit him too loosely. He was the epitome of what I'd imagine a used car salesman to look like, if a bit young, and I didn't expect to find someone like him on a luxury car lot.

"Hello!" The younger man gave Hunter a smile before smiling at me next. "How are you today?"

Hunter looked at the man and, without answering, turned toward the glass building. He'd slipped into his business persona, which could be considered rude at the best of times. Since it also meant power and money, though, people like these salesmen ate it up.

"I certainly don't need a car like this," I told Hunter in a quiet tone as we wandered toward the shiny Range Rovers on the showroom floor.

"Being that you haven't driven much in the last four or five years, I think safety is key." Hunter sauntered up to the nearest model.

"This is an extremely safe car," the salesman said,

shadowing us.

Hunter turned with a quirked eyebrow. He gave the salesman a hard look. "We need some time."

"Of course. No problem." The man gave a serious-looking nod. "Just let me know if you have any questions. I'll be right over there."

Hunter's arm slid around my middle. "It's safe, it's reliable, it'll get you out of the desert or mountains, and it is supposed to be extremely comfortable."

"I live in San Francisco, so deserts and mountains aren't really my concern. Hondas are reliable and safe and *inexpensive*. If you are determined to buy me something, why not that?"

"Do you not like the Range Rover?"

"Hunter, I don't need anything this extravagant!"

"How about an Audi? Mercedes?"

"I think you're missing the point…"

Hunter led me around the car and opened the driver's-side door. He pushed me toward the seat. "Sit in it."

"A Mini. Now there's a good idea. Small, fits in parking places, built well…" I peered into the sea of leather, inhaling the new car smell.

"I will not curl up into a ball to fit in a car."

"Who said you'd get to ride in my new car?" I stepped up into the car and wiggled into the seat. "Oh man." The leather molded to my butt.

"It is really big, though," I muttered as I looked behind me. The car seemed to stretch back to infinity.

"Let's look at the other models and see what you

think. Then, if you want something to compare it to, we can look at other manufacturers. I want you to be comfortable."

"I'd be comfortable in a Mini." I took Hunter's hand as I climbed out of the car.

"Within reason," Hunter amended, leading me to the other vehicles.

We didn't look at other manufacturers. We didn't even leave the showroom. What *we* did was look at all the models, each as awesome as the last, and then my involvement dropped away as Hunter decided to order one custom built. I had no idea why. I couldn't tell the differences between any of the models beside the appearance, and every one of them had more than enough whirlies and buttons for my needs.

After Hunter chose the features I "needed," the haggling began. The young salesman soon realized that he was out of his league and called in the manager. Two against one, and still Hunter dominated. It was pretty awesome, I had to say.

It wasn't until the end, when both men were staring at each other with hard eyes, that Hunter dropped the bomb. "I'll be paying cash."

A greedy sparkle lit up the manager's eyes. "Yes, sir. I'll see what I can do."

In the end, Hunter got nearly what he wanted, the salespeople weren't completely moping, and I was terrified I would crash this new and shiny automobile in the first month.

"What do you want to do now?" I asked as we left the dealership.

"Go home, order in, and make love to you."

I smiled like an idiot. "Sounds good."

WEDNESDAY MORNING AND I was looking around the office with shifty eyes. Hunter had indeed made love to me on Saturday, and then Sunday, and then Monday and Tuesday, too. He woke up and reached for me. He brought me in for nooners, and he tried to get some in the evening. It would be great, except he kept trying to finish without protection. He wanted to try for a baby.

Actually, he *was* trying for a baby. He was trying to make me lose my mind enough to forget about protection. Half the time it worked.

I should've been mad about that, probably. I'd said I wasn't ready, and he should respect that. The thing was, though…I kept thinking about how I'd forgotten the pill. My mind always went back to his mother's conversation, and about Hunter wanting kids. I couldn't help but wonder if I'd lodged that information in the recesses of my brain as code for *the time is now*, because I wasn't mad at Hunter. Not at all. I kept up my resistance, but I let him break me down on occasion. I let myself forget, and then reveled in his tender kisses and embraces.

I didn't know what I wanted anymore. Apart from Hunter, obviously. I wanted him with a passion that couldn't be natural. If love potions were a real thing, I'd look around his house for a cauldron and a pointy black hat, because that was what it felt like. Every time he came into a room I felt a smile bud, even if I was completely focused on something else. I sighed when he touched me and hung on his every word when he spoke.

I was annoying myself, but I couldn't help it. I was lovesick. It was ridiculous. But holy moly I did love that man.

"Stop thinking about the boss and get that report done," Brenda said as she set a cup of coffee on my desk.

Brenda looked down at me with a grin. "If you checked out any more, you'd have drool running down your chin."

I wiped my chin with the back of my hand, just in case, then reached for the coffee cup. "Sorry. He's just... Things are just weird right now."

Brenda huffed and went to her desk. "I don't know about weird, but I've never seen that man so happy. I don't even know him anymore. It's stressing me out a little."

"Maybe you'll take it as a hint to lighten up."

"Nah. Being grumpy works for me. Someone in this office has to scare visitors."

"Fair enough," I said, and with a flip-flopping stomach, I walked into Hunter's office. I'd decided that today would be the day of "no." I needed to get better at saying it. Since that first yes I'd been hopeless at standing my ground. Not so now. I would reclaim my ability to deny him.

"Hey, baby," Hunter said as he leaned back in his chair. He turned his body to face me.

"It still weirds me out that you say *baby*. I feel like saying please should come before pet names."

"Saying please has no effect on you. Saying baby makes you blush and your eyes sparkle." He watched me put his coffee on the corner of his desk before he reached out to me. "Come here."

"No." I got a zing of adrenaline. That was weird.

His brow furrowed for a moment and his eyes hardened. He hated when a flat *no* was thrown at him. I almost wanted to giggle.

"Come here...please," he said.

"No." I wrestled with my mad urge to laugh manically and run from the room.

He clasped his hands in his lap. His face closed down into a business mask, but his sexy eyes started to burn. "I want to kiss you, Olivia. Come here."

"No." I lifted my chin, unable to help a smile working at my lips. I turned and walked from the room. When I got back to my desk, I said to Brenda, "Sorry in advance."

Brenda glanced over. "Why? What did you do? You better not have quit, young lady, because I've never had it so easy in this office, and I don't know that I have it in me to go back to working hard."

"Nothing like that. I'm just going to tell him no a little more often."

Brenda groaned. "Is it too much to ask for a quiet

life?"

With the next round of coffee, I couldn't help a little saunter in my step. Keeping the smile away was even harder. I put the white cup on the corner, lining up the base with the little ring it had left behind. I was anal like that.

The *tick tick* of typing stopping. He swiveled in his chair. I risked a glance from under my eyelashes as I finished settling the cup. He was staring at me with his hands clasped in his lap. His expression was blank. He was trying to figure me out.

"Get me some water," he said.

"Please," I finished for him.

I walked from the room without telling him that I would. I was going to, of course. Saying no would be reserved for personal matters. He wouldn't fire me, but I didn't want to cause problems.

Brenda looked up as I passed by my desk toward the kitchen. "Did you spill, or did I screw up the coffee?"

"He wants water. He's trying to figure me out."

"Oh, Lord help him."

After getting the water and passing by again, Brenda said, "Be easy on him, Olivia. Men can't handle our insanity. They're too dumb."

I laughed as I entered the office. The *tick tick* stopped immediately. Hunter looked up, watching my progress. As I handed him the water, he didn't ask what my problem was, or if something was the matter, he just watched.

"You're welcome," I said, as though he'd said thank you.

He put the water on the desk. "I want to make love to you, Olivia."

I felt an almost physical tug to step closer to him. I swallowed down my immediate urge to say, "Yes, please!"

Instead, I took a deep breath, raised my chin again, and said, "Fantastic insight. But...no."

He clasped his hands in his lap again. The slow burn in his eyes turned to liquid fire. His shoulders shifted just a tiny bit, hardly noticeable, but suddenly I got the impression of power and command in his bearing. His ability to control a room was magical. And so damn hot.

This day of *no* might be harder on me than it was him.

He didn't say a word as I walked from the room. I could feel him watching, though. The silence pressed down on me in expectation. He was planning, working out my motives and figuring out how to get around them. He wouldn't force my acceptance; he'd *coerce* it. I'd just plopped an emotional chessboard onto his lap, and he was going to play it for all it was worth.

It was scary how well I had come to know the man in such a short time.

"This is kind of thrilling," I said in a breathy voice as I sat in my chair. My hands were shaking and my sexy systems were all revved up.

"What's his situation?" Brenda stopped what she was doing, turned to me, and took another sip of her coffee.

"He's intrigued, I think." I giggled. "It's weird, though, because if the roles were reversed, I'd be a mess of 'What has gone wrong? Is he going to dump me?' He's just trying to figure out how to get what he wants, though."

Brenda snorted. "Men and their egos. So he's not pissed, huh? I should've figured."

"No, not mad." I clicked into the report I should've finished by now.

"What are you trying to get?"

I shrugged, leaning closer to my monitor. "Don't know. Just...saying no."

Brenda barked out a laugh and turned back to her computer. "The two of you are made for each other."

"You should talk," I mumbled. "Before me, you matched his grumpiness exactly."

The next coffee delivery was uneventful. Hunter didn't look up from his computer. He didn't give me a command or ask anything of me. I could tell he noticed my presence, though. His eyeballs stopped moving. He had a page of words in front of him, and he was staring, but probably unfocused.

Tee hee!

Once again, I stopped myself from smiling. I turned and made my way from the room. As I walked out of the door, I turned my head just enough to see his desk in my peripheral vision. His body was pointed toward me.

"He must think I'm nuts," I mumbled as I sat at my desk.

Brenda didn't even look over. "You're not boring, that's for sure."

In the middle of the day I got a ping.

Hunter Carlisle: *Come in here.*

Olivia Jonston: *You forgot the please. Is this work related?*

Hunter Carlisle: *Yes. Per our verbal agreement, I need to fuck you.*

Olivia Jonston: *No.*

A few minutes later, he responded.

Hunter Carlisle: *Are you staying in the office for lunch?*

Olivia Jonston: *Yup. Want me to order something for you?*

Radio silence.

I stared at the conversation. Nothing happened.

I tapped my fingers on my desk, wondering what his game was. It wasn't like him to give up this easily. I also kind of wanted another reason to say no. It was making me excited and eager for when he finally worked around me and got his way.

How would he get his way?

"Stop giggling." Brenda reached in her drawer of menus. "Do you want food?"

"Read my mind. What are you ordering?"

"Hunter wants Japanese."

I leaned against the desk, incredulous. "He asked *you*

to order him food?"

Brenda frowned as she glanced up. "He always does."

"I just asked him if he wanted me to order something for him."

Brenda went back to her drawer, shifting through the takeout menus. "He probably knows you'd get the order wrong."

I didn't think that was it, but Brenda was right. I probably would. He had quirky tastes with some things, and I always felt bad with the overbearing and exacting orders, so I missed an item or two.

I looked back at the message. I stupidly wished he'd asked me, though. Or just...kept talking to me. It was a fun game to shut him down, but it also meant I didn't get to chat or touch him. I missed him.

"This lovesick issue is kind of annoying," I announced, pulling my report back up.

"Can't back out now. He'll win." Brenda held up the menu. "Want something?"

"It's irritating how well you know him."

"Uh oh. Sounds like this game has lost its appeal. Or were you apologizing for yourself earlier?"

I scowled at her, making her laugh, before going back to my report. "And no, thanks. He knows Japanese is my favorite. This has to be a no situation."

"Were these rules of yours pre-planned?"

"Nope, and I am starting to realize that my lack of planning is biting me on the butt."

"Yup." Brenda picked up the phone to order.

A new email came into my inbox. It was from Bruce. "Crap." I opened it immediately and looked over the contents.

"What?" Brenda loved to be in on all the action.

"We got a bug report from the geeks that tried out our game. What the *hell...*" I scanned the pages of problems. "How could all this have been wrong?"

"That's the thing with geeks. They're too smart for their own good. Now you know what it's like working with you."

"Hilarious," I said in a dry voice. "Can you order me some Indian, Brenda? I want to look at some of these."

"Sure. Are you going to escape to the conference room?"

"Yeah. Call this my lunch break."

"Got it."

Heaving a sigh, because I knew tonight would be a mess of frustration with this game, I heaved myself out of my chair and headed away from my desk. Games with Hunter would just have to wait.

Chapter 14

"INCOMING."

I looked up with bleary eyes before glancing at the clock. It was almost six o'clock. Brenda was buttoning up her coat and facing the elevator.

I saved the report I was finishing up. My mind strayed to the problems I still wanted to go over with Bruce's stuff. I'd knocked out half the list already. The issues were just tiny things, and some were already known quantities that Bruce was working on. Still, I was tired. Doing two jobs, for two tough bosses, was hard work.

A man walked toward us carrying a huge bouquet of sunflowers. Under his arm he held a big red box in the shape of a heart on top of a clipboard.

"Did I fall asleep and wake up on Valentine's Day?" Brenda asked as the guy came to stand in front of her desk.

The man set the flowers down on Brenda's desk and grabbed the red box and clipboard. "Uhhm..." He put the box down and ran a finger down the page on his clipboard. "Olivia Jonston." He looked up at Brenda.

Brenda pointed at me with a scowl on her face. Her gaze was accusatory. "Who's this from?"

The excitement of getting flowers and candies delivered was tarnished in that stare. "You didn't order them?"

"No." She moved closer to me as the man put the flowers and chocolates on my desk.

"Okay." The man raised his eyebrows and pushed out his lips, apparently asking if I was all set.

"Thanks," I said.

He nodded and walked away.

I grabbed the card among the sunflowers as a small bit of worry trickled into me. Unless my dad was back from the dead, the only person I could think of that both knew my favorite flower, and would actually send them, was Jonathan. Hunter would not like that development at all.

I opened the white cardboard. Inside was typed:

Love is not love
Which alters when it alteration finds,
Or bends with the remover to remove.
O no, it is an ever-fixed mark
That looks on tempests and is never shaken;
It is the star to every wand'ring bark,
Whose worth's unknown, although his height be taken.
   (Sonnet 116).
I love you. –Hunter

"What the hell?" I sat down as I stared at the note.

"Who's it from?" Brenda asked, leaning over me.

"Hunter."

"Hunter?" Brenda's brow furrowed in confusion. "Who'd he get to order them?"

A conversation fluttered in my memory. He'd once asked me to have sex with him on autopilot. He'd simply told me to go in there and drop trow. I'd responded that he should come out here with flowers and chocolates and recite Shakespeare.

I fell back into my chair, still staring at the note.

"He must've ordered them himself," I said.

Brenda was leaning over me, reading the note. When she straightened up, she was staring at me with wide eyes. "In all the years I've known him, that's a first." She put her hands on her hips. "I almost want to cry."

I laughed to try and hide that I was crying a little. "Me too." I wiped a tear from my cheek.

"Huh." Brenda went back to her desk. "That's sweet. He's a good guy."

"And he totally maneuvered his way into a *yes*." I ran my hand over the chocolates. They weren't even great quality; they were the silly, clichéd kind. And they were perfect.

I stood as Brenda grabbed her handbag.

"See you tomorrow," she said.

I made my way into Hunter's office. He didn't look up as I closed his door, nor when I locked it.

"How did you know sunflowers were my favorite?" I

asked as I came to stand beside his desk.

He typed a few things, clicked "save" in his spreadsheet, and pushed back from the desk. "I asked your mother if your father had ever bought you flowers. I figured he might have when you played dress-up. What else would you bring a princess?"

He stood and came around to me. His eyes were soft as he put his arms around me. "And I was right. Why sunflowers?"

"In the park where we always went to play and have picnics, there was this patch of sunflowers. It took me a while to realize their faces followed the sun. I thought it was so magical. I knew plants were living things, but that was like they had a brain, you know? At least to a six-year-old. My dad planted some in his backyard and I used to play in them all the time. It just became a *thing*."

Hunted lightly touched my lips. "Why were you saying no? Was it something I did?"

"So guys do wonder about that stuff…"

"Was it?"

I undid the buttons on his shirt, feasting on his delicious upper body. "You have a meeting in thirty minutes. We need to hurry. Kinda."

"Olivia?"

I undid the button on his fly and pushed down the zipper. "No." I reached in and captured his velvety shaft.

He sucked in a breath. "I like when you resist," he murmured against my lips. "I like the challenge. I know you'll give in eventually."

"You do, huh?"

"Now I do."

He backed me against the desk and lifted, sitting me on the edge. His hand worked up my inner thigh as his kiss hardened. Tricky digits grazed my panty-covered sex before stripping the fabric to the side.

"Oh," I sighed, opening my legs wider. He felt up my wetness before a finger dipped into my body. I moaned. My core tightened.

I leaned back and pulled at the back of his neck, making him lean over me. His body coated mine, hot and hard. His tip pushed at my opened before sliding inside.

"Hmm." I wrapped my legs around him, squeezing him closer.

He thrust. His manhood pushed deep into me.

"Let's not use protection this time," I whispered.

He paused for a second, probably making sense of what I'd said. Then he said, "God, I love you, Olivia. You give me the hope of a different life. A better life. Never leave me."

"Please..." I smiled against his lips.

"Please," he said softly. Lips still close to mine, he ran his hands up my chest and over my arms, pushing them flat onto the desk. He threaded his fingers through mine as his pace sped up.

I felt his urgency. His fire. His hips rocked into mine, his manhood inside of me taking all my focus.

"Oh, Hunter." I gyrated my hips up, taking more. A

new feeling scorched my insides before flowering, opening up, and spilling out. A love like I hadn't experienced before, one that could not be defined, took over.

We might be creating life.

Urgency took over my movements. Suddenly, something else was driving me. A different kind of love. I thought of a baby, of a family, of Hunter and me together forever.

I ripped my hands out of his and wrapped my arms around his shoulders. My kiss turned manic. I needed him with a desire I couldn't control.

"Take me," I urged. "Take me, Hunter."

His arms scooped under me. He lifted, picking me up before stepping out of his pants. I continued to rock, kissing him, as he walked us over to the couch. He dropped down, laying us down awkwardly. My leg was trapped by our bodies and my neck was bent awkwardly. He didn't stop, though. Still thrusting, harder, he pounded into my body, as desperate as I was.

"Floor," I directed.

He rolled, taking me with him. He crashed to the ground, me on top of him. I pushed off his chest, riding him. I rocked my hips forward, feeling the delicious friction.

"Yes, Livy," he said, his hands finding my hips. He lifted and then pulled back down, adding more force.

"Holy—" I bounced again, jarred with unspeakable pleasure. Over and over. Harder. "I'm getting close."

He sat up, wrapping his strong arms around me

again. "I love you."

"I love you, Hunter." I rubbed my taut nipples against his hard chest. His length worked in and out of me, winding me tighter. Driving me crazy.

"Oh yes. Oh God. Oh yes!" I squeezed my eyes shut, holding on for dear life.

We pushed through a plateau into unbearable pleasure. Our movements became smaller. Tighter. His muscles flexed against me. I bit into his shoulder, unable to push on but desperate to all the same.

"Come with me, baby," he commanded.

I exploded. Fractured. Color blossomed between my eyes. Ecstasy washed over me as he shook. Panting, I vibrated in the shock waves of one hell of an orgasm.

"Wow," I said quietly, losing all the strength in my body. I melted around him, laying my head on his shoulder.

"I hope you are pregnant, Olivia. I haven't been with you that long, I know, but it doesn't matter. I knew when I first met you, and despite trying to push you away, you just kept getting closer. This feeling I have for you will never go away, I'm certain. I just want to add to it."

"I know, Hunter." I kissed his neck. "Eventually we will."

"Maybe soon."

"Maybe."

Chapter 15

———∞———

TWO WEEKS LATER, my life hadn't changed much. I was still trying to use protection, and I failed most of the time. After a while, I wondered what the point was. If it was going to happen, it was. If not, that was probably good until I had known the guy for more than a couple months.

I needed to stop thinking about time frames. It made the situation sound totally crazy.

"Thanks, Bert," I said as he dropped me in front of my flat. I flicked my phone screen, checking the most recent updates to the game.

"I thought you were done with that game, Livy?" Bert said, waiting for me to get out of the car.

"I was supposed to be, but Bruce found something else. It's as if he isn't stacked with work in this takeover. *I'm* stacked with work."

"I don't know how you do it."

"I don't either. Okay." I pushed the door open and swung a leg out. Once out, I closed the door. "Bye."

I probably should've said the farewell before closing the door. Oh well.

Head still bowed over the game, I made it to my front door and reached into my handbag for keys. On autopilot, I let myself in and trudged up the stairs. At the next door, I did the same, only blinking out of my fog when the door lock didn't clunk over.

I pushed the door open and peeked in. "Hello?"

I stepped in and stared. Then blinked as I felt heat prickle the back of my eyes.

Pink scrawl ran up my wall. "Fuck you bitch!" Down the hall had more scrawl, graphic pictures, and other horrible things marring the beige. At my feet lay debris: glass, bits of wood, and pieces of what had once been a little ceramic elephant. Pictures had been torn from their frames and thrown about. Pots and pans littered the kitchen floor along with more broken glass.

"Livy."

I looked down the hall in a daze. Hunter was emerging from the bedroom with a stern look on his face. He'd left the office early, saying he had to run an errand. Janelle or Mrs. Foster must've called him.

"What happened?" I asked in a wispy voice, tears coming to my eyes.

"We've had a break-in. The police are on their way." He put his arms around me and hugged me to him. "It was Blaire, though I'm sure you guessed. I checked the surveillance."

I shook my head before resting my cheek against his

chest. "Surveillance?"

He kissed the top of my head before leading me to the living room. Once there, he cleaned off a spot on the couch and sat me down. Beside me was a large slash, revealing the cushion. The TV had a spider web of broken glass marring the face. The coffee tables, drapes—everything was ruined. She'd gotten to literally everything in the room and destroyed it.

"Blaire did some damage to my property as she was leaving. After she left graffiti here, I installed security cameras in the entryway to the building and the hallway. I planned to put them in here as well, but wanted to talk to you about it first. She beat me to it." Hunter's arms tightened. "We have her for breaking and entering, but not for destruction of property unless they run prints."

Tears overflowed as I looked at all my stuff. It was new, yes, but it was still mine. I'd claimed it. I'd called this home. Hunter's and my home. And now it was tarnished. I wasn't sure I'd feel safe after this.

"This isn't exactly a knife in the back, but it sure sucks," I said as I leaned into Hunter's warmth.

"I'm sorry, Livy. I thought I was absolved of her. With the contract out of my life, and her out of my house… I was naive."

"It's not your fault." I closed my eyes. "What does the bedroom look like?"

"We'll stay at my house tonight."

So ruined, then. She'd done the whole apartment. Not that that was a surprise.

"Do you have your project for Bruce saved in the cloud?" Hunter asked quietly.

"Yes."

"Good. She—"

I held up my hand. "Don't tell me."

The doorbell chimed. Hunter got off the couch and leaned toward the window. "The police are here." He went to let them in.

I looked around in misery. She'd gotten me right where it hurt the most. This had technically been Hunter's building, but it was *our* home. We shared everything. He spent more time in this place with me than in his own house. She'd broken into my refuge and plastered herself all over it in a way I surely wouldn't forget. I had no idea how she'd gotten in, which meant that even if we changed the locks, she could probably do this again. She'd tarnished the purity I had with Hunter.

The police came in, hard-eyed and severe. They looked around and started asking questions, but I didn't concern myself. Hunter would handle that. Instead, I texted Bert. I wanted to get out of there. Maybe I'd hit up the library until Hunter was done. I needed to think. I needed a new plan.

THE NEXT DAY I sat at my desk as the time clicked over to 8:00 p.m. I wanted to go home.

Where was home?

It certainly wasn't my flat at the moment. When I'd first walked in, I hadn't seen the extent of the damage.

That had changed when I had to walk through with the insurance agent.

The master bedroom had been the worst. My clothes had all been cut and ripped, as had Hunter's. Pictures were destroyed, the bed linen had been tossed out into the backyard, and she'd defecated in the middle of the mattress.

It was the last that I couldn't believe. She had pooped on my mattress. It was so far out there… I didn't know what to think.

I pushed myself up and made my way into Hunter's office. As I walked toward him, he glanced up, and then leaned back. He watched me sit across from him.

"Hey," I said.

"Are you okay?"

I shrugged. "Yeah."

"I pressed charges against Blaire. She's under house arrest until her trial. Her father is taking charge of her."

"I'm sure he's not thrilled about that…" I crossed my leg over my knee.

"No. More than that, though, he's embarrassed. He offered me his sincerest apologies. She'll be on a tight leash. You don't have to worry about her anymore."

I scoffed. "How can you be sure?"

"I let him know that if she comes within a hundred feet of you, she *will* go to prison. Also, if anyone that is in any way linked to her harms you, I will bury her or him. His business is faltering. I can give it a solid push." Hunter clasped his fingers in his lap. "I've made sure that he'll keep her in line or he'll cut her off. Blaire would never be able to function without money. She's out of your hair."

"That's good, but the damage has been done." I wiped a tear away.

"I'm sorry, Livy." Hunter took something out of a drawer and came around his desk. He knelt in front of me, holding a key. "Will you consider moving in with me? You can change anything in the house you want. If you need a room to yourself, you can have it. An office, your own TV room, anything. Whatever you want."

I smiled as my heart warmed. The flat had never really been mine—I knew that. I'd loved it because it was Blaire-free. Since that was no longer true, it had lost its appeal. What I wanted was to be with Hunter. I didn't really care where.

"Yes," I said, taking the key. "Okay, yes."

A smile lit up his face as he pulled me up and hugged me close. "I'm sorry it had to happen this way, but I'm glad of the final resolution. Let me close everything down and we'll go. I'll take you home."

Chapter 16

TWO DAYS LATER I let myself into my new home. Hunter's and my home. All traces of Blaire had been cleaned away. Her room was now a guest room. The places in the house she used to frequent were being redecorated. Anything she had bought or brought in was long gone.

My keys made a *clink* as they dropped in the bowl by the door. I headed upstairs to our room. Hunter had left work early to take care of some things with the flat and said he'd meet me at home. I figured he'd be in there.

Across the large room, the bathroom door was open. I could barely hear water slapping the base of the shower.

I wandered closer, stopping in the doorway. "Hunt—" I cut off as my gaze hit the counter.

The water shut off. The glass door rumbled on the tracks as it opened, showing the fantastically cut body of Hunter, wet and glistening. Heat rolled through me, and then extinguished as my gaze went back to the counter.

"I'm not even sure if I'm late, Hunter."

He grabbed a towel and rubbed away the wetness. "You're two days late, I thought you said. Last night...when we were watching TV..."

"No." My phone drifted down to my leg, the code I'd been looking at forgotten. "I mean, yes, I did. But I can't be sure because things might be different off the pill, so I don't really know..."

"And now we will." He motioned toward the pack of pregnancy tests. "I was afraid you'd sneak off and do it by yourself, Livy. I want to be here for it."

I gave him a pretty fantastic scowl. At least, it felt that way. Because I totally would have snuck away. I wouldn't want him hovering over me, watching the process. Not only that, but I knew he hoped the test would be positive, and I was worried he'd get his hopes dashed if it wasn't.

I also had to admit that mine would be dashed, too. I'd been thinking a lot about it. I was young, and it was early, but...something about it just felt right. A little reckless, maybe, but at least money wouldn't be a problem. The problem would be working hours. Both mine and Hunter's. But that would be an issue regardless, and he'd already identified it.

"I'm not going to get out of this, am I?" I said as he slipped his arm over my shoulders.

"I'm not going to push you, but..."

"You'll mope."

"I don't mope, Olivia."

I scoffed. "Say that to Brenda and see what she says."

Hunter kissed me on the temple before leaving the bathroom. "Brenda has a false view of things. I'll just be..."

"Waiting on the bed with bated breath, I know."

"My mother wants to have us to dinner soon, too. She wanted to check with your schedule."

"I—" I didn't get to finish. He'd closed the door behind him.

"So I'll just do this now, then, will I?" I said to the empty room.

I put my stuff on the counter and grabbed the test. I bit my lip, because I knew his look would be all kinds of sad when this came up negative.

I put my phone on the counter with the screen lit so I could still read the lengthy email Bruce had sent me, and took out the wand. I braced, holding it just right, and let go.

"Ew!" The stream hit off the side and splashed me. I angled. My shoulder hit my phone. The device went skittering across the floor. "Oh, come on!"

"You okay?" Hunter called through the door.

"A little privacy, please?" I yelled at him.

Muttering swear words, I cleaned myself up and fastened the lid on the test. There probably wasn't a romantic way to do this, but this was a bit ridiculous.

I reclaimed my phone and opened the door. Hunter was sitting on the edge of the bed in a pair of pants but shirtless.

"How'd it go?" Hunter asked as he stood. His stare fastened to the white plastic stick in my hand.

I wanted to say, "Well, I peed on myself, so what do you think?" Instead, because he didn't need the added stress of me being super stressed and really grumpy, I said, "Fine."

I sat on the edge of the bed. He sat down next to me. His gaze was still glued to the test.

"If it doesn't happen, Hunter, just know that it's okay. Okay? We don't—" I cut off as his expression turned to one of incredulous delight. I looked down at the little window. "Oh crap."

I wiped my forehead and then my eyes. I stared at the little plus sign. "Kimberly said coming off the pill and immediately getting pregnant was highly unlikely…"

Hunter took a few quick steps into the bathroom. When he came back he was reading the package. Apparently "+" wasn't a dead giveaway to him. The package lowered. The biggest smile I had ever seen on Hunter's face.

I was struck mute. Transfixed. In that moment I couldn't imagine anyone, ever, being more handsome than this man. Adonis had nothing on this guy.

"We're pregnant, Livy!" He threw the package on the bed and bent to me, scooping me up into his arms. "We're pregnant!"

I felt my own smile blossom. I had life inside of me. I was going to be a mom. Hunter was the father of my baby!

He put me down gently. His lips connected with mine, deep and passionate. I lost myself in the feel of him, his safety. I ran my hands up his chest as his arms hugged me close. When he backed up, his sexy, smoldering eyes stared down into mine. For a brief moment, I saw a flicker of doubt. A hint of fear. But then they started sparkling again over his beaming smile. "I love you so much, Olivia Jonston. This is the best day of my life. Thank you."

He bent and scooped me up into his arms again before carrying me downstairs and into the living room. He settled us both on the couch, the same place I'd said I was late. His fingers threaded through mine as I snuggled against him.

"Promise me something, Livy," Hunter said after a quiet moment.

"What's that?"

"Promise me you'll bear with me, okay? I know it's mine but...I have ghosts haunting me. Please don't be offended or sad if I ask you if it really is my baby. Or if I have times of jealousy. I won't mean them."

"I know, Hunter. I might yell at you anyway, though."

He squeezed me affectionately. "That's okay. As long as you stick by me. There is only one of you in the world—I'd be lost without you."

We'd been through a lot of turmoil, Hunter and I. From my misgivings, to his, we'd worked around contracts and made it through his father and Blaire. We'd earned this moment. We'd earned our future together as a family. I couldn't have been happier.

The End

The story concludes in the fourth book:

Forever, *Please*

Chapter 1

"COME IN HERE." Hunter passed by my desk with a determined stride. His palm slapped the door, pushing it wide as he went into his office.

I looked over at Brenda with comically wide eyes and a thin mouth. "Sounds like I'm in trouble..."

"I'll say. What'd you do?"

I got up and grabbed my notepad, just in case the bad mood wasn't directed at me. I didn't have high hopes. "Not sure."

"Close the door," Hunter said as I made my way toward him.

A thrill arrested me. My breath quickened. Since moving in with him two months ago, we hadn't partaken in much office fornication. He usually just left work earlier and went home with me. He wanted to take his time. I was all for being bent over the desk, though. Since finding out I was pregnant, he'd been too gentle by half. I needed a good rogering.

"You wanted to see me?" I asked with a grin. I stood beside his desk.

"Sit." He leaned his elbows against the desk. The light from the windows behind him showered his broad shoulders. His sexy, hooded eyes trained on me. I marveled at his handsome face, with its strong jaw, straight nose, and lush lips.

I was the luckiest girl in the world to be able to kiss those lips. To feel his firm touch and reap the benefits of his clever fingers. There was a list a mile long of girls that wanted him, but he'd chosen me. I didn't have to understand why; I just had to bask in the glory.

"Your game goes live tomorrow, right?" Hunter asked, his gaze dipping for a brief moment, touching my stomach. "Come here."

"I—huh?"

He stood and reached for me. "Come here and sit on my lap."

I smiled like an idiot. I bounced up and grabbed his hand. He reeled me in before sitting on his chair and settling me onto his lap. His lips grazed my neck as his palm covered my belly. "How are you?"

I laughed with the change in his tone. "I'm good. Kind of tired. The baby blogs say that's normal, though."

"That's what I wanted to talk to you about. You're doing too much. You have shadows under your eyes and you're dragging."

I tensed. "Hunter, I haven't had much choice. We had the final push for the app these last few weeks. We're good now, though. The marketing is all set up, the game is loaded, the bugs are worked out—we're ready. Now I can relax."

"Bruce says you have another project coming up. You have more levels to design for this game…"

I got off his lap. I couldn't help my testy tone. "You're my boss in this job, Hunter. You're not my boss with the side project."

"It's my job to look after you and our baby, Olivia. You're doing too much. It has to end."

I snatched up my notepad. He'd been saying this for the last few weeks. Over and over he harped on about the amount of work I was doing, but at the same time, most of it was for him. By the time I finished all of his tasks, it was late. Then I could do what I loved, which was working for Bruce. In order to break this cycle, I had to choose. One job or the other. Hunter knew it, Bruce knew it, and, unfortunately, I knew it too.

The problem was that the one that paid well, and was with the man I loved, didn't interest me. My favorite part of the day was working on Bruce's projects. Most of the new levels were my design. Bruce was starting to step away a little to come up with the next great thing while I took on the future of the current game. I even had an idea for a game of my own.

I shook my head and started for the door.

"Olivia." The deep, commanding voice dripped down my spine and pooled in my lady parts. I slowed despite myself. I loved when he used that tone. It did things to my body that should be illegal.

I turned to him, raising my eyebrows in a silent question.

"I love you. Good luck tomorrow." He turned to his computer.

Warmth spread throughout my chest. My heart surged.

I left the office, wondering where my irritation at his talk had gone. The man could knock me off balance way too easily.

"Did you get in trouble?" Brenda asked as I sat down.

"Kinda. Same old thing—I work too much."

"That's rich, coming from him."

"I know, right?" I scoffed. I'd found my irritation again. "He works more now than before—" I snapped my mouth shut. I was about to say "before I got pregnant." That was a big no-no. All the blogs and books said it was best not to tell anyone before the three-month point, when the chance of miscarriage dropped significantly. Besides that, I wasn't married, hadn't known Hunter that long, and didn't have one thing in my future figured out. There were more than a few reasons not to spread the news around yet.

"What is he doing so late, anyway?" I asked as I turned to my computer. "I tried to spy on him, but his calendar is locked up tight."

"He had me block it off for structural organization. Probably trying to fit the pieces of that new company into this one."

"Huh." I squinted at my company email. Seeing that nothing new had come in, I checked my personal email on my phone. Three new messages, all from Bruce.

"What was that sigh for?" Brenda was facing her computer.

"You're nosy."

"You're more interesting than my job."

I read the first message, then the second, then rolled my eyes on the third. "Bruce is just as demanding as Hunter. He wants me to complete a bio for our website."

"You have a website? What's it called? I wanna look."

"It's not live yet. For a guy who just sold his business, Bruce is hellbent on jumping right back into the fire."

"At least you like the work."

I couldn't argue with that.

I pulled up the report I was supposed to be working on, but my brain kept sliding sideways. First it would go to Bruce's emails. Then I'd think about the game I wanted to design until my thoughts returned to the baby.

It wasn't just me using this body anymore.

Holy crap, I'm pregnant!

I worked on hiding my smile. If Brenda randomly glanced over and saw it, she'd ask what I was so happy about. Being happy was sometimes a personal affront to her mood.

I still couldn't believe it. I was going to have a baby. With Hunter Carlisle! Karma was shining on me; that was for sure. I didn't even care that he'd gotten way overprotective. Given his past, he was forgiven.

Letting a small smile curl my lips, I tried again to focus on my work.

AT EIGHT O'CLOCK I rolled my shoulders and sat back, totally drained. My eyelids drooped and my body felt completely depleted. This growing a human thing was taxing on the energy front, I'd say that much.

I took a deep breath, checked my phone, but ignored the little red button on my email. I'd bet those six messages were all from Bruce. The man couldn't consolidate. He'd think of something, fire off an email, think of something else a moment later, and fire off another. Apparently a notepad for ideas leading to a summary was too much to ask.

I walked into Hunter's office. When he noticed me, he glanced at the clock at the top of his desk. His lips turned into a thin line.

"Don't say anything," I warned. Not waiting for an invitation, I walked directly to him and draped myself across his lap. I flung my arms around his shoulders and buried my face into his neck. "It won't help."

"How much work do you still have to do?"

"For you, or for Bruce?"

He paused. "This isn't working, Olivia. We agreed to stop working so much when we had a family. Our family starting quickly doesn't negate the need to slow down."

"I have six months to slow down. Let's just get this release out of the way, and then I'll have less to do. A couple more days and I'm in the clear."

"What do you have to do for Bruce tonight?" he asked as he softly ran his fingertips down my back. His hands pulled on my silk blouse, untucking the ends from my skirt. His palms ran up the bare skin of my back.

"Little things, I think. By the time you're done here, I'll be done."

"I might be late. I have a couple meetings."

"I didn't see any on your calendar..."

His fingers glided over my bra strap. A quick tightening and then my bra loosened. His hand slid over my skin until he reached up and cupped a breast.

I moaned as my nipple tightened under his palm.

"I'm just trying to square everything away. I foresee a few late nights hammering out a new direction for the company."

I let my head fall back as he kneaded my breast. "Does that brain ever shut off?"

His lips traced a trail of heat up my neck. "How are you feeling?"

"If you're asking if I'm feeling good enough to bend over your desk, I absolutely am."

His hand dropped to between my thighs. I spread my legs as my breath quickened. His fingers traced down the middle of my sex before pushing aside my panties. He rubbed in the right spot.

"Oh, Hunter." I put pressure on his chin, turning his head my way. I nibbled his lips as a digit worked into my body. My core wound up, needing him.

I put my palm on his cheek and deepened the kiss. My tongue flirted with his as his finger sped up. His thumb worked lazy circles around my clit.

"Oh." I sighed against his lips, gyrating clumsily while still on his lap. His pace quickened, rubbing and thrusting. My body started to burn. My moans intensified.

"Oh, God. I'm going to—" My words cut off in a hasty release of breath. Shivers racked my body as pleasure coursed through me, setting me on fire. I spasmed with the climax before melting in his lap.

After I'd come down, Hunter stood me up gently. His body pushed against mine, trapping me against the desk. His kiss became insistent as his palms worked up the outside of my thighs, lifting my skirt. I wrapped my arms around his neck, lost in the kiss. In the feel of him.

He turned me around. A palm in the middle of my back had me bending. I heard his belt jingle, and then felt his blunt tip against my opening.

"Hmm," I said as my eyes fluttered closed.

That tip applied pressure, parting my folds. I braced, expectant. His hard length entered me slowly, so large. The breath rushed out of my lungs, everything focused on the searing pleasure that worked into my body.

"Yes, Hunter." I bent over further, wanting more.

His chest lay against my back as his hips met my skin. He held himself inside me before backing out slowly.

"Faster," I begged.

He complied. With a hard thrust, he entered me completely. I moaned, pushed against the desk.

"Let me know if this is uncomfortable," he said softly, his voice shaking slightly.

He pumped into me again, and then again, his movements becoming frantic. I braced against the desk, my eyes closed, as pleasure ran through me in waves. My core, already warmed up, was now in overdrive, soaking up each thrust in ecstasy.

"Yes, Hunter," I said. I gripped the edge of the wood, focused on that pounding pleasure. On the friction. On his body inside mine. "Oh, yes."

I rocked my hips in tiny movements, adding just that bit more. The feelings now overwhelming. The sensations pulling me under.

"Oh God. Oh my God. Oh—" Everything tightened up. My toes curled.

"Oh!" I blasted apart. Intense wave after wave rocked through me. The orgasm stole my breath as Hunter quaked over me.

His hands slid down my arms. His fingers threaded through mine as we came down, panting over the desk.

"I promised myself I'd be more careful with you," he whispered.

I turned my face toward him until his lips were glancing off my cheek. "The human body isn't that fragile, Hunter."

"Still. I don't want anything to go wrong, Olivia. I don't want you or the baby put in any kind of danger."

If I wasn't mistaken, there was a tiny plea in his voice. His past was trying to encroach on this conversation, I had no doubt.

I straightened up. I knew a moment of regret when his body left mine—something that never seemed to go away—before I turned around and put my arms around his neck. "I'm good. I need a little bump and grind every so often."

He gave me a lingering kiss. "Okay, off you get." He helped me straighten up my clothes. "I don't want you awake when I get home. You need your rest."

"What time are you coming home?"

"A couple hours, I think."

I gave him a flat look. "That's more than a twelve-hour day, Hunter. I'm not the only one who agreed to work less…"

He kissed me on the forehead. "Off you get." He gently nudged me toward the door.

I should've argued, but those orgasms put me over the tired cliff and I still had work to do.

I dragged myself to my desk, packed everything up, and headed home. Once there, I grabbed the dinner out of the oven, went to my office, and opened my personal laptop. Time for job number two.

I just hoped all this work was going to be worth it. Tomorrow would be the moment of truth on if we'd wasted our time or not. Unfortunately, tomorrow would also be a deciding factor on my future involvement. If this took off as Bruce said it would, I'd have some hard decisions to make, because Hunter was right—I couldn't keep this up. I had two full-time jobs. I'd have to choose, and I wasn't sure that I was going to choose Hunter.

32600025R00140

Made in the USA
Middletown, DE
10 June 2016